Ivy

PRIDEFUL MAGICK COLLECTION
BOOK ONE

TENTH ANNIVERSARY EDITION

HOLLOW RYAN

Ivy

Second Edition

Published by Hollow Ryan

Ebook ISBN: 978-1-968729-01-1
Trade Paperback ISBN: 978-1-968729-00-4
Hardcover ISBN: 978-1-968729-02-8

Cover elements courtesy of:
Vintage Damask by DarkMoon_Art via Pixabay.com
Realistic Smoke Fog by Hakan Kaçar via Vecteezy.com
Vine is Growing on a White Background by Yui Nakamori
via Vecteezy.com

Cover Design by Christiana Nehmsmann
Interior Design by Christiana Nehmsmann

Books By Hollow Ryan

Prideful Magick Collection

Ivy
Oleander
Valerian
Hawthorn
Avens

Demon Kin

Demon Kin: The Queen
Demon Kin: The Lovers

TABLE OF CONTENTS

For Mariah Wilson

The first to experience Lex's journey with me.

Chapter One

A HOUSE IN NEW ENGLAND

The house was the most beautiful I had ever seen. Three stories of aged brick wall, narrow windows with quaint little arches over them, and chimney after chimney crowning the dark roof. From the driveway, I could see the wooden door that had a distinctive Colonial design. It made the house seem more dignified.

A winding, stepping-stone path had sunken into the earth over many years of use as it led from the front gate to the house. The stones were wide and smooth and I admired how they were sort of pieced together like a puzzle as it made its way across the lawn. Bright flowers framed the path all the way up to the front door where bushes stood on either side like protective knights. It was a new addition to the landscaping, I could tell, and one that had won over my mom's interest.

Yet, neither age nor garden could ever be considered my favorite part.

Covering the dull red brick was a thick, tremendous layer of ivy. Spreading across the entire right side and most of the front of the house, it only seemed to thin toward the top. Someone had carefully kept the vines pruned away from the windows and doors, but had not bothered to keep it from crawling for the sky like a spider in the corner of a room, spinning her web so that she may watch all below her.

The ivy flourished in a way that all of other plants in the garden could not hope to achieve. Even the climbing roses trailed lazily along their wood picket fence, growing as far from the other plant as possible. Tulips hid from view and the daffodils were just tall enough to bloom. Even dandelions refused to grow out on the welcome green lawn, as if they knew they would be smothered in the ivy's shadow if they dared. None of the plants were able to match the ivy.

Except maybe one.

It was a bush, just inside the garden gate.

Fuzzy-looking brown arms extended and came into bloom with what looked like golden-yellow tentacles. A breeze blew through the yard, setting the odd plant to waving wildly. Just as enthusiastically, the ivy waved back.

Witches hazel. Even as I thought the name, the yellow tentacles waved cheerfully at me. For some reason, it made me feel uncomfortable and I quickly looked back at the house.

This is how a house in New England should look. Exactly like this; brick walls, numerous chimneys, and ivy that reached to the heavens, creating a layer of concealment for its inhabitants. Dark green leaves faded into lighter green. Occasionally a splash of red would streak through the climbing vines. It was beautiful. *This is home.*

"Alexandria Marie Ryder!"

At the sound of my mother's voice, my head whipped around as my face arranged itself into an expression of innocence. She must have been calling my name for a while if she was using my full name now.

"Are you going to help us with these boxes or not? Why don't you get the door for us?"

Turning from the garden gate—when had

I moved over here?—I ran up the stepping-stone path to the beautiful wooden door. Pushing it wide, I held the door open so that my parents could trail past me with boxes piled high in their arms.

When the train of boxes finally stopped, I was released from door duty and instead given a more enjoyable task. Laughing, I ran through the house and pulled the dusty white sheets from the furniture. Couches and tables. Lamps and chairs. Upstairs I gasped in delight as I removed the largest sheets from the massive canopy beds and wooden wardrobes. For the first time, I wasn't disappointed in my parents' choice in choosing to rent a fully furnished home.

It was almost as good as moving into a castle, being in a house with the air of history so thick that I could feel it settling around me like a blanket. With the grand furnishings and aged architecture, I could imagine myself in old, pretty dresses, running around and becoming part of a different time. Nowhere else had my imagination ever been touched like it was being prodded here.

Night had long since fallen by the time

we stopped working. Far from being finished, it would take another two days of serious unpacking before we were fully settled into the old house. But already it felt like home. A place I could easily see myself staying in forever.

Later that night, when I finally found myself in my new bedroom, I trailed across the wooden floor to the window. I pushed open the casements and stuck my face out into the night breeze. Closing my eyes, I breathed deeply the smell of the last of the August air.

When I opened my eyes, it was just in time to watch a fluttering leaf tear itself away from the foliage wall that clung to my house. Instinctively, I reached out and snatched it from the sky before the breeze could carry it away. Cradling it in my palm, it suddenly felt as if my fingers were tingling. Smiling widely, I trailed back to my bed. Climbing beneath the covers, I placed the ivy beneath my pillow and fell into a contented sleep.

I left the window open.

Chapter Two

BLACK CATS AND SHATTERED GLASS

My mother drove me to school the following Monday. It had taken us all weekend to finish unpacking, but we were soon settled. I'd only missed the first week of school at Cedar Creek Elementary. It didn't make me any less nervous. Butterflies fluttered around in my stomach and it felt like one was in the back of my throat, making it hard to speak. Dragging my feet, I followed my mother slowly into the building.

I was abandoned shortly afterward. Once I'd been handed over to a teacher, my mother left. She had to get to work, I knew, but I still did not want her to leave me. However, at nine years old, I was at the age where I refused to admit fear.

Maybe being a Marine's daughter helped me.

My dad was a lifer. Military born and bred, enlisting at the young age of eighteen. He wouldn't be able to handle a life without extensive orders, given and taken. His new promotion was the whole reason we were in Cedar Creek. He'd finally decided that he had had enough of moving his wife and child to base after base, and instead settled us in a home as far from military life as we could handle.

"You're the new kid, right?" whispered the girl I shared a table with.

I smiled at this expected title. "My name is Alexandria. But you can call me Alex." As I was taught, I stuck out my right hand. The girl stared at it in surprise before finally shaking it. Her handshake was weak and I had to keep myself from making a face. Maybe she was left-handed.

"I'm Rebecca. Call me Becky," she whispered.

"It's nice to meet you, Becky," I responded, a wide grin spreading across my face. I had successfully made my first acquaintance in Cedar Creek Elementary.

My morning passed easily. Having Becky to help me was a real blessing. I'd been to a few new schools in my young life, but this was the easiest yet. At lunch, I sat with Becky and her friends. I was introduced to Mark, her neighbor, and Nathan, who was Mark's cousin. Amy was Becky's best friend.

After lunch, we all headed out for recess. The playground was covered with kids from our own grade as well as those in the two grades below us. Kids ran around, playing tag and hide and seek, while my new friends and I strayed toward the fence. We could see the woods beyond the chain links. Mark, Nathan, Amy, and Becky all stood talking to one another. For a long time, it seemed, I was–gratefully–forgotten.

Suddenly, out of the shadows of the trees slunk a small, dark figure. It came toward the fence in a slow walk, one tiny paw in front of another. I crouched down and stuck my arm through the fence, my tiny fingers stretching out to the cat. Black as coal, the feline possessed strangely bright green eyes. They were like em-eralds or jade, staring at me with a coldness like stone, but comforting all the same. I felt my fin-gers slide into the black fur, the cat leaning its head into the palm of my hand.

I heard gasps behind me but ignored them

for a moment. Only when Becky took a step forward was my petting interrupted. The cat pulled back, its fur rising in a spiky array, its lips pulling back as it hissed at my new companion. A frown fixed itself on my face. The cat didn't like Becky. What did that mean?

"Alex," Becky whined as the cat took off into the trees again.

"What?" Her shocked and scared expression only confused me.

"That was a black cat," she whispered in a frightened voice.

I shrugged. "So? What's wrong with a black cat?"

Becky just shook her head.

"Black cats are cursed. They're witches' familiars," Amy hissed, not sounding too different from a cat herself.

"You seriously believe in that stuff?" I scoffed. All eyes were wide as they looked at me. Becky looked scared stiff.

"Don't make fun of them, Alex!" Amy snapped. "They're real! There's one that lives down on Old Grove Road. That was probably her cat."

"There is not," I heard myself say. What were they trying to do? Scare me? It took more than some old ghost stories to frighten me.

"Fine, don't believe," Amy sniffed. "But when you get cursed, don't say we didn't warn you."

I walked away from her. It was ridiculous. Curses and witches? Please! How could they be so naive? Just looking at them made me glad that recess was over and we were herded back inside.

I was still thinking about the cat and Amy when we finally got to art class. We were each given a little mirror and told to draw ourselves. I tried my best, but the face on my piece of paper didn't look anything like me. With all the lines I had seen in the mirror, it made my face seem like that of an old woman. My head was hung in failure as I waited until the last bell rang. Gathering my things, I stood up in a hurry.

As I stood, I managed to knock the mirror off of the table. Everyone stopped still as the object hit the floor. The glass broke into a hundred pieces. Fifty images of my shocked face stared up at me. My dark brown hair pulled back in a barrette; my blue eyes, wide in surprise; and my small mouth, opened wide in shock. All I could think was: *Seven years of bad luck*. Staring at the shattered glass, I suddenly felt cold.

Chapter Three

JUST A DREAM

When I got home that afternoon, I couldn't help but be a little superstitious. After all, what were the odds? A black cat. Breaking a mirror. All the way up to the house, I tried not to step on the cracks between the wide stepping stones. Finally, I walked through the door with a relieved sigh.

Leaving my coat in the cupboard beneath the stairs, I took my backpack to the kitchen where my mom was humming. As I walked in the door, I saw an older version of myself. The same dark hair ran in wavy lengths down my mother's back. The same blue eyes spotted me in the doorway. A smile, with my lips, spread across her face. Really the only thing she possessed that I did not was a nice, white, even smile. But I would have that, too, someday. Dad already said I could get braces when I was twelve.

"Hey, baby. How was your first day?" I frowned involuntarily. "That bad?" she asked, brushing my hair away from my face. I shook my head.

"Not really. I made some new friends. Becky, Amy, Mark, and Nathan."

"Then what's with the long face?"

"Mom, what happens when you break a mirror?"

My mother stared at me, her face slightly perplexed. Suddenly, she laughed. "Is that old saying still making the rounds then? I remember hearing it when I was a girl. 'Break a mirror and you'll have seven years of bad luck.'" She mimicked the words but that did not help. My expression didn't change and she leaned down to kiss my forehead. "Relax, baby. If you break a mirror, you just have to clean up the glass."

I smiled, relieved. My mom would know. She knew a lot of things. I trusted her. Besides that, what did Amy know? It's not like the cat was fond of her any. Maybe it just knew that she was afraid of it. Animals could smell fear. The poor cat wasn't to blame for her being scared of an old wives' tale.

"Thanks, Mom."

"No problem, sweetie. Do you need my help with anything?" She was noticeably eyeing my book bag. I nodded and we sat down at the kitchen table. We each ate a bowl of fresh fruit salad as we did my homework.

That night, I lay in my bed, staring at the shadows on the ceiling. I wasn't afraid anymore. Not of school. Not of cats. And especially not of broken mirrors. Maybe I wasn't totally ready for the next day of school, but that had nothing to do with fear. Amy was a brat. A spoiled one. Becky, too. I'd noticed that as I was lying there, thinking about how the day went. The way they acted was not a way in which I was comfortable being around. My dad always told me to choose my friends wisely. Had I already chosen wrong? Maybe I'd find someone else to play with on the playground tomorrow. Someone else to sit with at lunch. That would fix things ... maybe.

I don't know how long I was lying there, unable to sleep. Hours passed. My parents had long ago gone to bed. A few times, I tossed around, kicking the blanket away from me. Then I would get cold and fumble around before pulling it around me again. Finally, my eyes began to drift shut and my breathing slowed down a little.

Just as I was about to fall asleep, a strange noise made my eyes shoot wide open. My heart started to beat faster as I laid in bed, straining my ears to hear the noise. There it was again! I slowly got out of bed and walked to my bedroom door. Easing it open, I winced when it creaked. Now, as I listened, I could identify the noise.

It was music. Piano music. Quietly, I drew nearer the sound. Down the stairs, turning left, and into the parlor I went. As I entered the sitting room, the music suddenly stopped. I gulped. The ivory key had been pressed down only a moment before. Now, the last, lonely note hung in the air, echoing over and over in my ears.

Suddenly, I heard a high-pitched giggle! A shadow moved by the piano and I took a step back out into the hallway. In that one second, I could have sworn that I saw a little girl. Before I could hear or see anymore, I turned on my heel and ran all the way back up to my room. I just barely stopped my door from slamming shut before launching myself into my bed.

It was just a dream, Lex. It was just a dream.

Chapter Four

OLD GROVE ROAD

The next day at school, I barely remembered the worries that had kept me awake all night. So what if Becky and Amy were stuck up? So what if Mark and Nathan hardly talked to me? It wasn't like I cared. I had more important things to worry about. Like, maybe I really had been cursed. Stupid mirror. Stupid piano.

No matter what, I still refused to believe that the cat had been the cause of all this. Rather, it was Amy who was the troublemaker. She had been nothing less than a brat about the whole thing. Poor cat. If only it knew what had happened to me since it had shown up.

"Earth to Alex!" sang Becky in my ear. I jerked upright, realizing that I had been nodding off.

Stupid piano. I hadn't been able to sleep all night long.

"What?" I asked before I noticed that the classroom was almost empty.

"C'mon," she said. "It's lunch time." Together we got up and headed for the cafeteria.

Despite their many attempts to talk to me, I found myself often ignoring the group I was sitting with. My mind was still full of piano music and a girlish laugh in the middle of the night. Only once did I think, *Who is she?* I instantly threw that thought aside. Some things were not worth knowing about.

"What about it, Alex? You up for it?" Amy asked snidely.

That brought me back to their universe. I looked around, blinking in surprise. "Up for what?"

"Going down Old Grove Road. There's a lake where all of us go swimming. And you won't be scared. You know, since there aren't any witches," she sneered at me. I felt my pointed chin lift automatically and met her muddy hazel eyes.

"Sure. Where is it? I can meet you after school on my bike," I answered, not once thinking any of this through. I was being challenged. The Ryders did not back down from *any* challenge.

Mark and Nathan helped to draw a map of the town for me, giving me specific directions to the corner of Norfolk Street and Old Grove Road. School passed quickly after that. At least it gave me something else to begin obsessing over.

Once the bus stopped at my house, it took only a few moments to convince my mother of my plans. Not wishing to hold me back, she even helped me pull out my bike from the shed it had been stored in. Glad to see that the chain was rust-less and the tires aired up properly, I was off down the gravel driveway and out onto the road.

Old Grove Road was easy to find. Much easier than I had previously thought. My new friends obviously could not judge distance properly. Where they said I would have to travel a mile and a half along Norfolk Street from my own road's corner, it turned out I had but one mile to make it to the proper corner.

Looking at the empty dirt road, I waited by the sign acknowledging its existence. Old Grove Road wasn't like other roads in town. Sure, some were made of the same red-brown dirt. But others had houses between the trees, driveways parting the cedars and pines as one traveled along. Homes could be glimpsed through young saplings and the voices of dogs and children could be heard out on the street. Not on Old Grove Road.

Large, shady oak trees lined the entire road. They were spaced evenly, each growing tall enough to paint the sky each morning. Between them grew saplings of different natures and trees too stubby to compete at all with the earthly giants.

Right at the corner, across from the old, rickety sign, was a flourishing apple tree. The smell of rotting apples traveled across the road in a sickly sweet fragrance. Nothing smelled as sweet as newly rotting apples.

It was taking too long for my friends to come. I noticed that after ten minutes, they should be there on their own bikes. Not one of them lived very far from my own house. I knew that from the bus ride. So where were they?

Maybe they're not coming.

For only a second I thought this might be true. But then I thought of Amy.

She was dying to see my reaction to the road

and supposed witch's house. Which meant she wouldn't give up until I either faced it or ran away screaming. My Ryder family instincts kicked in. With a firm sort of determination, I stood up on my bike and turned it toward the dreaded scene. Letting the shadows of the oaks overwhelm me, I pedaled up the empty Old Grove Road.

Chapter Five

COTTAGE IN THE TREES

I don't know what I was expecting. Maybe they were going to jump out of the bushes as I began pedaling down the empty road? Perhaps they'd yell and laugh, glad to have delayed me as long as they had. Or, if they were truly scared, they'd try and get me to turn back. None of that happened, however. Nope. I just kept pedaling.

The road got darker the farther I went. The oaks stayed the same exact distance apart, like it really was in the middle of an old grove of trees, but the young trees between had had time to grow up. Pines and maples spread out in the September sunshine. More apple trees sent up the fragrant smell of fruit left for the animals. Once, my nose even stumbled on the smell of mint; meaning that one of the bushy plants alongside the road was hiding the fragrant herb from view.

All around, the Earth painted portraits of greenery and life. The last we would be able to see before autumn slipped into our world and changed our perception of what lay around us.

Farther and farther I went down Old Grove Road. Half a mile had gone by, I was sure. Maybe they meant it would be a mile and a half before I reached the lake where they swam? It didn't matter. I kept going, enjoying the peace of the leisurely ride.

Only once did I look back. It made me wish I had a camera with me. The long road, framed on either side by stupendous trees, had branches arching over it to create a tunnel of sorts. And there, at the very end, a bright light as the shadows gave way to Norfolk Street. Mysterious.

I'm not sure when it happened. A strange feeling just kept inching over my body. Once, I shivered, causing the bike to wobble in protest. The shiver passed, but my pedaling became less determined and more leisurely now. I was at least a mile down the old dirt road by now. And I hadn't once seen anything to make me afraid.

Certainly nothing supernatural had occurred, giving even less weight to their suspicions of a witch in the area. But the feeling grew stronger the farther I went.

Then I saw it. There, peeking out of the trees, was a familiar slinky creature. The black cat from school. Jade eyes stared at me with that same stone-coldness. I still found that gaze to be comforting. My bike slowed to a stop and I climbed off. As I kicked down the kick-stand, the cat turned and disappeared into the brush.

"Wait!" I called. Too loud. All around me, the trees seemed to be listening, injured at having heard such a loud voice when they had been used to whispers and silence. My head ducked automatically as I felt ashamed. Why I felt ashamed, I don't know.

Before I thought about it much further, I had run to where the cat had disappeared. Suddenly, I could identify the feeling that had been coating my ride: tranquility. As I neared the house, I'd been tranquil. I'd felt a sense of rightness and comfort. Staring at the small cottage in the trees, where the black cat had run to, I pondered my lack of fear. This place, so obviously the home of

Amy's supposed witch, did not fill me with anxiousness or adrenaline. It filled me with peace.

"So, you finally made it," Amy's whiny voice came from behind me. I turned to see all my acquaintances riding toward me. So that was the plan. Amy wanted me to reach it before them. Well, she wasn't going to get a laugh or jest out of me.

"Yes," I said with a bright and cheery smile. What was so wrong with the place?

Mark's face was pinched together as he stopped his bike near Amy's. It was shaking underneath him, he was that nervous. Becky, having ridden up beside Amy, seemed to be inching farther and farther away from the house, down Old Grove Road. That made me think there really was a swimming hole down at the end. Else, Becky would have been inching backward like Nathan was doing. Not one of them could sit still. Even Amy was edging around on her bike, her foot at the ready to push off and pedal away. My smile made them all look at one another.

"So? What do you think?" Becky demanded. Her eyes were wide with fright, darting between me and the little cottage. I turned back to study the home of their supposed witch.

The cottage was made of large fieldstones, plastered together in the old way. From the way it looked, it could be as old as some of the oak trees in the area. Purple-gray smoke curled upward from the single chimney, giving notice that the roof, at least, was only a few years old. Not that my companions paid any attention to that. Nor did they notice the overgrown tire marks that marked the driveway that stretched far beyond to the back of the house. Probably to fill up a large propane tank that probably provided her with heat in the winter and fed a gas burning stove. Some people just didn't think of these things.

"Well?" Becky snapped once more.

I shrugged as I turned back to them. "It looks pretty normal to me. Why should I believe a witch lives here?" They all stared at me, mouths agape.

"Didn't you see the cats? Or the gargoyles? And look here," Mark suddenly exclaimed, pointing to the garden gate—left ajar by my feline friend.

Looking where he pointed, I finally saw the

things that *I* hadn't noticed. Along the ground, just where the gate would cover it, were it shut, was a pure white line of salt. It was thick. Meant to be seen. And there, on the posts holding the gate in place, rested two small gargoyles. The little stone creatures looked like the ones on old churches and cathedrals. Their bulldog-like heads held their mouths open, stone teeth exposed to frighten off intruders. Instead of being afraid, I saw them only as guard dogs. Like a dog, I suddenly felt the urge to pet one.

Before I knew it, I was standing before the gate, hand lifted and fingers tentatively touching the gray stone. It was cold to the touch, the shadows of the trees protecting it from the warming sunlight. Smiling, I stood up on my tiptoes in order to stroke it's smooth head as I had stroked the fur of the cat. Suddenly, that same furry feeling was against my ankles.

Looking down, I saw the same black cat with jade eyes slinking through my legs, pressing its warm body against me. I'd worn tan shorts, intending on actually having to swim with these kids, so I could feel every hair that brushed against my skin. I laughed happily, just watching the feline.

"Alex!"

The cat and I both looked up into the astonished faces of the other kids. Amy's eyes looked about to fall out of her head. As my jade-eyed friend looked up at her, it hissed and frayed up as it had done to Becky only a day ago. Amy took a step back. With one last turn about my legs, the cat sped back through the gate, pushing it open even wider. I took a step toward it instinctively. Suddenly, a hand was gripping my arm, just above my elbow.

"What are you doing?" Nathan hissed, surprising me greatly. I thought he was the biggest chicken of them all, staying back the way he did.

"Going inside."

With that, I slipped out of his grasp, pushed open the gate, and took a step over the defined salt line.

Chapter Six

MAIDEN, MOTHER, CRONE

It was wrong. In my head, I knew that to be true. I was trespassing. This thought filled my nine-year-old stomach with a flutter. My dad would be so disappointed if he saw me now. Shame flooded through me and I thought about turning back. But the damage was already done. I'd crossed the line. I may as well sate my curiosity while I was already shaming the Ryder name.

Only once I'd crossed the line did I realize why Mark had used the plural form when he'd asked if I'd seen the cats. Just beyond the gate, an orange and white tabby slunk out from under a low, vibrant green frond. Then there was an ashy gray, sitting in the windowsill of the stone home. On the step before the quaintly arched door was a black tuxedo cat, with white socks and underbelly. Its tail, with the white tip, bounced fitfully beside him as he flicked it every which way. For some reason, I got the feeling that he was not in the least bit happy to see me.

My own feline friend was sitting off the dirt path on a low, stone bench. She sat squarely in the middle, on top of some engraving in the stone. Since I couldn't see what it sat on, I looked at the legs, where more stone carvings embellished the white surface. On the left side, facing away from the bench, was a young girl. A maiden with a youthful face. The right side, also bearing up the seat of the bench, held an old woman. Her back was hunched beneath her cloak, her face lined, and she leaned on a long staff.

As I studied the figures, my feline companion jumped off of the bench, revealing the engraving in the stone. At first, all I noticed was the pentacle in the center. The five pointed star surrounded by a perfect circle. Then I realized that there was a woman carved there as well. She cradled the star, where her abdomen was, and her face was aged with maturity, while not so aged with infinite wisdom as the other woman.

When I realized what they were, I began to look them over further. The maiden was just a girl. Maybe a little older than myself. Her waist-length hair hung in waves down her back, flowers threaded through the stone mane. With her face tilted up and away from the bench, toward the sunshine, it was at first hard to realize why she looked so familiar.

The same nagging sense filled me as I turned to look at the old crone, again. Her face, too, seemed strangely familiar. Like I had seen that particular pattern of wrinkles before. Or seen the same small threads of loose hair hanging in someone else's face not long ago. Sighing, I turned my attention to the last, yet middle, woman.

Suddenly I gasped. It was a familiar face I now beheld. Full lips, curved into a kind smile. Almond-shaped eyes, only slightly darker than the stone surrounding it. Hair that flowed over her breasts and around her swollen stomach—pregnant with the pentacle. High cheekbones, with a single dimple showing on the left cheek of the woman. It was my mother's face. My face.

I looked again to the maiden. There I was again! My pointy chin, my button nose, and even my own dimple in the left cheek. The maiden in the stone was me in only a few years to come.

Looking at the crone, I was no longer unsure as to where I'd seen her face. I had drawn those lines in art class. I'd seen that face in the mirror I was destined to break. Right before me was my own future. A look I would embrace many years from now. It was so clear how my face would age that I had seen it before I'd even had the evidence before me.

"Alex!" I heard the harsh whispers behind me.

All of them had called my name in low whispers from the second I'd crossed the salt line. But only now did their words pierce my own frightening revelation. Still, I couldn't look at them. My future was set in stone and I could not take my eyes off of it.

"Alex, c'mon," a voice suddenly hissed in my ear, making me jump.

All of a sudden, Nathan grabbed my arm again and began dragging me from the garden. Before the bench was lost in the sea of flowers and herbs of the garden, I took one last look at it. Only then did I notice the small tendril of ivy, enwrapping the stone in caressing locks of greenery.

Nathan continued to drag me out. As we passed through the gate, the last thing I noticed was our footprints scuffed through the white salt line. Again, a feeling of shame overwhelmed me. It was my fault her line was ruined. And as I pulled my eyes away, all I saw was the black cat sitting just on the cottage side of the ruined white line. *I'm sorry*, I thought, as if the cat or its master could hear the words.

Chapter Seven

FIRELIGHT

I didn't bother to keep track of my bike ride home. My mind was filled with too many conflicting images. A black cat. Jade eyes. Broken glass. Shadows and piano keys. My face, in three different stages of my life. My face in fifty pieces of broken glass. An ivory key depressed by nothing. A haunting melody swirling in my head. Music traveling up old stairs that creaked with each wrong step. And a single vine of ivy. All of this tumbled around in my brain, making everything else simple details.

My afternoon was gone. Shock took up most of it. That night I ate dinner with my parents and then headed immediately to my room with the simple claim of forgotten homework. In truth, I never touched the history paper that was due Friday. Instead, I sat on my bed, letting my eyes trail over my still new room.

The room had a sort of blocky, sideways L shape to it. My bed was a double—much better than my previous twin size—and pushed almost against the eastern wall. It was an old canopy bed. White see-through—my mother called them *gossamer*—curtains fell out in waves from the thin wooden beams above me.

On either side of my bed were nightstands. A lamp was on the one farthest from the door, closest to the northern wall. The other held my alarm clock and a small vase filled with flowers from the garden. (My weekend contribution to my own comfort.) One of my most favored books rested next to the lamp. The book that was as old as I was, entitled with my mother's loving hand: *Ryder Pride.*

The north wall of my room held a single window overlooking the front of the house. Ivy teased at its edges, the wind breezing through and throwing their tiny shadows across the glass. A single translucent curtain fell over the glass, bordered by rich blue drapes, which my mother was sure to close at night. As I had the window open to the fresh air, the sheer fabric fluttered in the breeze, billowing out as though it were a maiden's favor being offered to a valiant knight. The blue curtains fluttered lazily, their heavier fabric saving them from the antics of their gossamer counterpart.

The only piece of furniture against that wall was my desk. The aged wood matched the canopy bed. Perhaps it was made of maple or cedar. Part of me suspected that the solid wood was nothing less than oak. Just like the large bookshelf that rested beside the desk on the west wall.

Also on the west wall, across from my bed, was my very own fireplace. Not that it would be used before I turned the very mature age of thirteen, or so my dad said. Personally, I knew myself to be very mature when it came to fires. However, I also respected my father enough not to contest his decision.

My bedroom door was placed between the original west wall and a secondary eastern wall. This was the cause for the backwards L shape to the room. Two doors were on this wall. One led to my quaint closet. The other to my own bathroom. It had been an addition to the old house once indoor plumbing had been invested in. A private bathroom was an unexpected blessing for someone of my age.

Having made this examination of my room multiple times, my heavy eyelids began to droop. Thanks to the ghost music of the night before, I hadn't gotten any real sleep. It was still an hour before my bedtime when I closed the window, breathing in the comforting smell of thriving ivy for the last time that day. As the filmy curtain fell back into position, I attempted to draw closed the heavy, royal blue drapes. Failing due to my lack of height and maneuvering capabilities, I gave up and crawled into bed. Mom would get it when she came in to say goodnight.

There were orange flashes on the other side of my eyelids. My eyebrows pinched together in a confused way. The flashes danced beyond my line of vision. Flickering rapidly, they would die away with the same amount of speed, letting the darkness fill in the gaps they had left. Only to be replaced by another wild, flame-colored flash.

Flame-colored. Flames. *Fire!*

My eyes snapped open in the light, my dark and gloomy room seeming much less dark and gloomy than it should. Swiveling my eyes around, I could only see my closest southern wall and part of my ceiling from around my thick blanket. However, from what I could see, the shadows were writhing away from the orange lights that danced on the walls. The canopy had a strange, amber cast to it. I gulped.

It took all of my meager courage—and much more of my impertinent curiosity—to force me to inch back the blanket. Slowly, ever so slowly, I eased up onto my elbow. Then my hands shot to my face to wipe sleepy seeds from my eyes. *I must be dreaming!* There, in my private, little fireplace, a blaze danced cheerfully. For a long, long time, I could only stare at the whirling orange figures in the flames.

Normal girls would have screamed. *I* should have screamed. But from a very young age I had been taught that screaming was wrong. So it was out of the question, even now.

Time passed. Whether slow or fast, I couldn't tell. The fire continued to dance. Flashes of color continued to throw themselves at my walls and across my furniture. After a time, my eyes became unfocused. I was tired and my body wanted me to lie back down and go to sleep. But I could not stop staring at the fire in my room.

All of a sudden, a disconcerting creak filled my ears. The noise did two things to me. First: it made me realize that the fire dancing in my fireplace was utterly silent. No cracks of wood or sparks flying through the air. It was truly silent. Second: the noise filled me with absolute terror. My heart pounded in my chest and my palms became slick with sweat. And yet, I still had to look. Instead of rushing under my blanket and hiding there until morning, my eyes slid to the corner of the room where the sound had originated. I gulped, and turned my head.

Translucent as fog, an empty rocking chair moved forwards and backwards, straight through my chair and part of the desk. The creaking couldn't even be drowned out by the pounding in my ears. Unwillingly, my eyes filled with terror-induced tears. Just as suddenly as *it* had appeared, so did she.

The little girl who liked to play the piano.

My mouth fell open as I looked at her misty complexion. She didn't look at me. Her eyes were trained on her hands, neatly laced together in her lap. The skin was as white and luminescent as a pearl. Her auburn curls were pushed back by an intricate hair band in the middle of her hair. From there, they tumbled down to her little shoulders.

Clothed in a party dress that reached to her knees, she seemed comfortable, despite how it was filled out with puffy layers of fabric underneath the ivory top layer. Even the sleeves had a puffiness to them. Gold-edged designs were inlaid on the fabric of the dress, giving it even more of a luxurious appearance. White stockings covered her legs, and tiny white shoes were on her feet. Without noticing anything, she just kept rocking in the chair. As I studied her, my heart became just a little calmer. She didn't seem so bad.

Then her eyes snapped up to meet mine and my entire world went black.

Chapter Eight

THICKER THAN WATER

Come morning, I realized I had fainted. It only made my subconscious lie that much harder to believe. Even in the darkness, I had tried to convince myself that it had all been just a dream. Now, as I woke to an empty fireplace and no sign of a rocking chair of any kind, I was almost willing to accept that I had an overactive imagination. If only I had woken up in a normal position, instead of sprawled out in a heap as if I'd been casually dumped on my bed by a stranger.

It goes without saying that I kept my strange nights to myself. My logical, military-kid brain chalked it all up to sleep deprivation and the excitement of our move to Cedar Creek. The next logical step was to remove the bad influences that caused such disturbances. Of course, it was easier said than done.

I started with the one that, perhaps, intimidated me the most. As I sat down to eat breakfast that morning, I looked up at my mother with wide, innocent eyes. In the sweetest voice I could manage, I asked her something I never thought I'd ever speak of.

"Mom? Can you teach me to play the piano?" My whole goal was to rid myself of bad influences. Including any fear of shadows and pianos with self-moving keys.

My mother stood there with her familiar perplexed expression. She always had that look whenever something I did or said baffled her. All the same, she answered slowly and thoughtfully, "Lex, I don't know how to play."

"Oh," I said, letting my face fall. I stared at the breakfast in front of me, not looking up. It probably wasn't good to be proud of your ability to manipulate your parents. But I was proud at the ease in which my mother responded to my expression.

"I can look around. There has to be a piano teacher *somewhere* in this town," she said. My answering smile spread across my face, accenting the single dimple in my left cheek.

"Thank you, Mom!" I replied, jumping up to hug her. In little time, I finished my breakfast and went out to wait for the bus.

As I walked along the stepping-stone path, I could smell rain in the air. The clouds hung low in an endless gray sheet. So low were they, I wondered if the oaks down Old Grove Road were brushing through them or if the pines that pierced the sky were forcing the clouds around their pointy ends. Our trees reached toward the sky, their leaves turning upward in expectation.

They and I were on different ends of the desire scale.

What happened to the sunshine? Where was the heat of the last true summer days? Why was all this cold and damp moving in at the worst time?

As I stood waiting at the gate for the big, yellow bus, my eyes focused on something just as yellow. The witches hazel moved in the wind, tossing branches about and waving its tentacles in the air. Instinctively, I reached my hand out, letting the gold tendrils brush against my palm.

A bumblebee hovered nearby, trying to get the last of the pollen it could reach before hunkering down for the rain. Keeping still, I waited until it passed on to the other side of a large bush.

When the bus pulled up, I opened the gate and forced myself to be ready for this complicated school day. Since our friendship was only going on day three, I was hoping it would be rather simple to sever the ties I had forged with the two girls and male cousins. They were not the type of people I would have been proud to introduce to my parents. Therefore, they were not people whose company I would seek.

Again, this was easier said than done.

When Becky and I sat down at our shared table, we both did a tremendous job at pretending neither one existed. I felt like my friendship with Becky might be able to melt into a simple business-like relationship. As long as we were civil to each other during class assignments, I saw no reason that it could not work.

When lunchtime came, however, it complicated things. As I sat at a table, by myself, I watched with a small smile as Becky directly avoided me. Whatever she thought of my stunt at the cottage in the woods, it obviously made her wish to steer clear of me. Amy, too, avoided any form of communication with me. This made me sigh in relief. She was not someone I could ever truly get along with.

As the boys entered the cafeteria, it became apparent that my luck would not hold. Mark, I thought, would be easily gotten rid of. His ties to Becky were beyond any form of independence I had witnessed from him. Nathan was a different story. Almost without thought, Nathan spurned the seats by the girls and took up one across from me. This decided Mark. Blood was thicker than water, apparently. So it was that both boys were sitting across from me, acting as if there was nothing strange in their seating arrangements. It bothered me.

"Why aren't you guys sitting with Becky and Amy?"

"You were really brave yesterday. Either that, or really stupid." Nathan's voice was calm as he shrugged. I raised my eyebrows in surprise.

"Amy and Becky are way too chicken to do what you did," Mark added in a boisterous tone. Like he wasn't ready to pee himself just standing in front of the cottage.

"You never went that far," I snapped. I hated liars.

"Someone had to stay with the girls." Mark conveniently ignored my scowl.

"Why'd you go in, Alex?" Nathan murmured, glancing around the room for potential eavesdroppers. Amy and Becky glared at us but I turned away from them.

"Because I wanted to. Why did *you* come in?" I demanded.

"To get you out," he snapped in response to my tone.

"I didn't need you to get me out. You ruined her line, you know. The salt had your footprints right through it," I answered harshly.

"You were in the witch's garden and you only care that I ruined her salt line?"

"Yes. I was perfectly safe. Maybe that line was important to her. If she really is a witch, it might have been used for something." Unwittingly, I had begun to play their little guessing game.

"*If?*" scoffed Mark. "You saw the gargoyles. And what about all them cats? Only a witch has that many cats."

I turned my little button nose up at him, vexed. "There were only four cats that I saw. And liking gargoyles does not make someone a witch. I like them and I'm just a normal girl."

"There's nothing normal about you, Alex. Nothing."

It was just after he said that that lunch was concluded and we headed outdoors. I was allowed to go my separate way at that time. Of course, I just headed back to the chain link fence by the woods and thought about what Mark had said.

Maybe there *was* nothing normal about me. Wouldn't that explain the way things were lingering around me? Superstitions were growing on me like the wild rose that grew on our fence, covering the entire thing in fragrance and thorns. Is that what was being done to me?

Was my lack of normality what made me susceptible to being harassed by a young ghost? Is that why black cats liked me and no one else? Did it make me knock over a mirror, shattering the glass into many different pieces? My life; was it the reason my future was written in stone, my face making up three different women in a mortal timeline? Mark was right. In no way was

I, Alexandria Ryder, *normal*.

Chapter Nine

WHAT'S IN A NAME?

The rain started to fall before I reached my house. It was a light, misty rain. The kind I hated most. Water pricked at my sensitive skin, making me wince. Was it too much to ask that—should it *have* to rain—it be a real downpour? Downpours I liked. Dad and I always went out and danced, getting soaked straight through to our skin, whenever there was a good, hard rain. But misting air and falling tears were no fun. They were just depressing.

Maybe that's why, when I entered the house and glanced into the parlor, a shiver ran up my spine as I looked at the piano. It could have been the pricking water on my face or sticking to my coat. Perhaps it was the chill throughout the house, the heat not being on to warm it. More than likely, though, it was my flashback of the past two nights. A little girl with auburn ringlets, who probably played the piano with great skill for her age. I wondered again what had happened to her. Again, I banished the thought.

Ghosts, witches, and curses are not real, I thought angrily to myself. After stomping out of my boots and shoving my coat into the cupboard, I headed for the kitchen where my mother was making me an after-school snack. Together we washed up some grapes and ate them at the dining table as we once more went over my schoolwork.

My history project was soon complete. A whole day before it was set to be turned in. That meant, barring another assignment, I would not have anything to worry about tomorrow after school. I was just pondering my options when my dad got home.

After we hugged, I was given a present. The book he handed me was thick and heavy, filled with pictures upon pictures of the area we lived in. Cedar Creek's history was in my hands. Along with detailed maps and prominent residents. It was perfect.

With my father home, I took the book up to my room and left it on my desk. Then I trailed back to the kitchen and began to help my mother with dinner. Unfortunately, my present was soon forgotten. My mind automatically reverted back to everything I'd experienced since moving to Cedar Creek.

I admit, I was afraid to go to bed that night. After dinner, I lingered in the family room with my parents. When my bedtime was only moments away, I sighed when my mother insisted on taking me upstairs and tucking me into bed. Though I didn't argue, I dragged my feet every single step of the way.

Once we entered the bedroom, I went to change into my pajamas and brush my teeth. I knew that my mother was securing the window and closing the curtains. After this was all done, I slowly walked toward my bed, casting little glances at the northwest corner and the fireplace. My mother then tucked me in and turned to leave.

"Wait," I called out before she could make it to the door.

"What is it, baby?" she asked, walking back

toward me. I slid to the side, patting my bed with a little, innocent hand. I was manipulating her again. This time, I didn't care. I needed someone with me tonight.

"Stay with me awhile? Just until I fall asleep?" I begged. For a moment, my mother just stood there.

"Just for a little while," she nearly whispered. Stretching her legs out on top of my bed, my mother leaned back against the many pillows. I instantly curled into her side, tilting my head just right as she began to stroke my brown hair. For a moment, we laid there in silence.

"Tell me a story," I suggested. My eyelids were heavy. Maybe a story would distract me from my nightmares.

"What story would you like to hear?" she asked, a smile in her voice.

"Tell me how I got my name," I suggested. It was one of my favorite stories because it was a love story with a happy ending. My mother chuckled, casting a surreptitious glance at the book on my nightstand.

"Again?" I nodded. "Very well, then."

She took a minute to grow more comfortable

on the bed, squeezing me tighter into her side. There was no way for her to know how much I appreciated that. How much I needed that. Once she was comfortable, she rested her head on a pillow and stared at the top of the canopy as she prepared to tell me the story.

"Once upon a time," she began, causing me to giggle. It happened every time. "A confident, brash young man had just graduated from high school. His name was John Ryder, and he was aching for an adventure. Friends of this inquisitive young man encouraged him to go abroad for the summer. The last summer he would have to follow his own orders before he entered boot camp in the fall. Our young Mr. Ryder agreed."

I loved the way her voice flowed. The words she used and the phrases that went with them reminded me of when she used to read Jane Austen books to me. My eyes drifted closed as I lost myself to her story.

"With fire in his heart, and passion in his blood, Mr. Ryder set off across the great Atlantic Ocean, searching for a tale worth telling.

"At the same time, a girl from humble roots was thinking deeply about her college plans.

Her freshman year at Brown was only a summer away. Three short months would see her behind its aged doors, walking its respected halls. Companions and family members of her own urged the young woman to shed the shy country-gal persona she had cultivated in her home town. *They* knew that she was destined for greater things. With promises of literature, history, and knowledge of the past did they finally wrest this young bird from her nest. For the first time, Melanie Warren was forced to spread her wings and fly." She paused here, as she did every time she told this story, to check if I was asleep.

"Keep going," I murmured. Her low chuckle filled my ears and I snuggled even closer to her, turning on my side while she stroked my dark mane.

"Miss Warren was lured first to the streets of London. For many weeks, she explored and learned all she could of England. Next, she traveled to Wales and Scotland. Ireland held much of her interest while she was resting upon that island.

"Only when her curiosity was sated there did she travel to fill her mind with the lore of

France and the poeticism of Spain. All across Europe our fair heroine traveled; with only two dear companions, Sofia and Yvette, traveling the long roads with her. Finally, as her careful and precise planning had dictated, their trip through Europe had come to an end. The only place left that was close to Miss Warren's heart was the richly beautiful land of Egypt. Without protestations, the three companions soon set their eyes toward the great pyramids and vast sweeps of the Valley of the Kings." I looked up at her, making sure she would know to continue the tale; that I had not fallen asleep just yet.

"Months had passed since our dear Mr. Ryder had left his home, in search of something even his own heart hid from him. So, like the fair Miss Warren, Mr. Ryder found Europe to be quite to his taste. More time passed in the immensely different cultures than he thought could have possibly slipped away.

"As the month of July was drawing to a close on the Mediterranean Sea, our dashing young hero made a bold decision. He would leave behind the still uncharted lands of the European continent. Instead, he would follow the route of the great rulers and warriors before him. Roman legions and Greek heroes had taken the path he was determined to travel. Yet, whereas the wiles of an Egyptian woman had often been the conqueror of powerful men, Mr. Ryder was determined not to be so defeated.

"Following in the footsteps of the famed warrior, Alexander the Great, our valiant hero set his eyes upon the flourishing city of Alexandria. It was one of many cities named after its conqueror. However, few kept the name after his demise. Leaving the Egyptian Alexandria to revel in her own, personal glory.

"As luck would have it, our lovely young maiden was also drawn to the beautiful Alexandria. She was filled with awe at the ancient sites that survived the ravages of nature. *He* wished only to walk the same streets as the men of power had walked before him. She sought history and understanding. *He* thought only of the way these great men had been treated. How society had spread their arms and welcomed them to their hearts, though they had been defeated by them. Of course, perhaps he should not have been in Egypt were that the image he wished to sustain.

"On one particular day, fate decided to throw these ill-matched people together."

"And you fought over where you would go," I said with a yawn, hiding my mouth in my covers. My mom stroked my hair again.

"Yes," she whispered. "There was a tour company, targeted specifically toward Americans. As it turned out, Mr. Ryder and Miss Warren were forced to mix company. However, the choice of location was, as yet, undetermined. A poll of the group did little in the way of making a decision.

"It was the desire of Miss Warren and, she assumed, her companions to visit the Biblioth-eca Alexandrina. The Library of Alexandria. She wished to discover as much as she could about the city before she was due to return to the United States. Where better than the place where the histories were kept together?

"Mr. Ryder, however, scoffed at the idea of being cooped up in a library. His time abroad had not been for intellectual enlightenment. Rather, he searched for things that would make his blood rush fast and give him a kick of adren-aline. His choice for such extremities? Well, in Alexandria, his only hope was the *Catacombs of Kom el Shoqafa*. While Miss Warren was discouraged by his reasons, she could not deny that the Catacombs were often considered one of the Seven Wonders of the Middle Ages.

"Seeing his opposition crumbling before his eyes, our daring hero made a preemptive strike. Observing a fair, lovely young woman before him, he did what any man would do. Graciously and courteously, he offered to take the young Miss to the library the following day, if she would but agree to two conditions. It was said in such a way that our poor heroine was forced to accept both conditions before hearing them spoken aloud. The first, she knew, was her reconciliation of the Catacombs venture. The second condition caught her completely by surprise.

"Having found himself in such a winning position, Mr. Ryder was quick to take advantage of his situation. At once, he sprung the second condition on Miss Warren. He asked for a social engagement after their visit to the Bibliotheca Alexandrina. And what do you think our poor Miss Warren did when she learned what she had agreed to? Why, she did nothing more than blush so deeply that her face was the scarlet of a luscious rose petal. Yet, she had her honor to maintain. She had given her word and would not recant.

"Mr. Ryder and Miss Warren spent the following day together, exploring the library filled with its unrelenting history. Afterward, our dashing male treated the young woman to dinner. Despite intentions, the two young people found themselves deeply attracted to one another from that night on.

"As time would have it, they returned to the States, each going their separate ways. The only thing keeping them connected were the letters they wrote. These words kept them close and drew them closer. When they were finally able to meet again, Mr. Ryder surprised her more greatly than he had ever done; he proposed. The rest, as they say, is history. They married and had a healthy, beautiful, amazing baby girl. When they discussed what to call the child, they decided to name her after the place where their story had first begun. And so Alexandria Marie Ryder entered their lives. There she shall ever remain."

Chapter Ten

A SILLY DARE

I wasn't sure whether I had still been awake for the end of the story, or if I'd just continued it in my dreams. This had been my bedtime story since long before I understood the words. My mother had even written it in my first journal. It was the story of their beginning and mine.

When I woke the next morning, I realized that having my mother with me had kept the ghost away. Her being with me had kept the little girl from waking me from my dreams. Although, if I was being honest, my deep sleep could have had more to do with my exhaustion. At the same time, I liked to think that the comforting arms of my mother, and her soothing voice, had kept away my curse for one night.

As we ate breakfast, we watched the morning news on the small TV in the kitchen. Today was supposed to be mostly cloudy with scattered showers. Tomorrow would be cloudy. And Saturday and Sunday were supposed to be filled with sunshine. That just about made my day.

Heading out into the garden, I made sure to watch my every step. The rain had left the stepping-stones slick. All around me, the freshly washed plants sent up a wild array of fragrances. There was no way to identify all of the different flowers and bushes adding to the combined perfume.

Reaching the garden gate, I turned and looked back at my new home. *This is how a house in New England should look.* That thought hadn't changed. Only now, after spending nights being tormented by its past, did I realize how exactly it fit in its surroundings. This house had a history. Just like the land it rested on.

A history that was reaching out to me with a magnetic pull. That girl with her tumbling auburn curls and dress that was made for a holiday or special occasion. I had to wonder about her. If I didn't, then she would continue to give me sleepless nights. Something had to be done.

My thoughts were interrupted by the arrival of the bus. Passing through the gate, I strode up the steps and headed for the very middle. I sat down and took another lasting look at my house. As I watched, the wind flew across the yard, shaking the ivy in an almost violent manner. That was the last I saw as the bus pulled away.

Two stops from mine, we picked up Mark and Becky. Amy got on with them, making me think she'd spent the night at Becky's. Unfortunately, the two girls each sat in a seat close by mine, almost directly across the aisle. I tried to ignore them.

The bus continued and picked up a few more kids. One of those stops was Nathan's. He got on with his older brother, Tyler, who immediately flew past us to get where the middle schoolers sat. Nathan moved toward the middle, where some of us 'bigger' kids sat, who weren't in middle or high school yet. He stopped right next to my seat and looked down at me.

"Can I sit with you?" he asked quietly. The girls had gone silent and I watched Mark's mouth drop from the corner of my eye. I shook my head violently and Nathan turned to sit with his cousin, as he normally did.

Suddenly, their talking and laughing reached a high pitch. I had the bad feeling that I was at the wrong end of some joke. Almost immediately after I thought this, Becky turned to call my name. I couldn't help but wonder what had happened to our mutual silence. Slowly, I turned away from the window to look at her. Amy and Becky were both grinning widely. Mark had a small smile on his face. Nathan was staring out his own window, ignoring the four of us.

"Hey Alex, do you really not believe that there's a witch on Old Grove Road?" This came from the kid sitting in front of me and I turned to look at him. He had shaggy brown hair that fell into his dark eyes, framed by the most beautiful eyelashes. No matter his appearance, I instantly didn't like him. Instead of being genuinely curious in my opinion, he was mocking me.

My jaw jutted out stubbornly as I said, "No. I don't."

"See, Ryan," Becky giggled. "We told you."

"Alex is too worldly for small-town ghost stories," Amy commented with a bite.

Now, if it was the first day of school, I would have agreed with her wholeheartedly. As stuck-up as it made me sound, I had experienced much more of the world than these kids. And that experience had given me a logical, confident mind.

But it wasn't Monday. It was Thursday. And things had happened since that first day to make me begin to believe in ghost stories. As Amy laughed at me, I felt my jaw relax and the blood drain from my face. I launched into my argument before Ryan or the others had time to notice.

"I never said I didn't believe you were serious about being afraid of her," I snapped. "I just said that I'm not sure that she's a witch. You have no proof. Why should I believe you?"

"So, you're willing to believe as long as you get proof?" Ryan asked before Amy could say anything. Her mouth was open wide in indignation and she looked about ready to start screaming at me.

"Yes. As long as there's proof," I qualified.

"Alright, Alex. Then why don't *you* get proof?" Ryan asked, a stupid grin plastered all over his face. From the corner of my eye, I saw

Nathan turn his head in our direction. I ignored him, my chin lifting at Ryan's challenge.

"And how do you propose I do that?"

"Go to her house. And go *inside* the gate," he challenged.

In that instant, I learned that he didn't know. Becky and Amy hadn't gotten around to telling him yet. Turning my head slowly, I smiled widely at the two girls. Then I turned back to Ryan and said with confidence, "That's a silly dare. I've already done it."

Ryan's mouth fell open and he looked to my snide ex-companions. They both nodded unwillingly. Mark, too, told him I had gone into the garden. Nathan saw me looking at their seat, and leaned forward to catch my eye before turning back to the window. I made a snap decision.

"Nathan did, too." Everyone looked at me. Including Nathan. Ryan's eyes were swiveling between him and me like he couldn't believe it. "He came into the garden to get me because I was busy looking at something." A sudden memory of the bench made my voice falter.

"Alright, Alex," Amy finally said in her high-pitched whine. "If going inside the gate is a silly dare, then what do you say to knocking on her door?"

My Ryder instincts were too strong to question the answer.

"I accept."

Chapter Eleven

A DEEP BREATH AND...

From the second I said it, I could feel the butterflies in my stomach. My Ryder instincts and my Ryder conscience needed to get it together. One refused to let me back down, while the other condemned my actions in not doing so. It was wrong to bug a poor old woman just because all of the kids in the neighborhood believed her to be a witch. Yet, wrong or not, I was the one who insisted on proof. And I would be the one to get it.

My school day only got worse from there. Becky, Amy, Ryan, and Mark all spread it around our grade how I was going to knock on the witch's front door. After hearing about it from a kid at lunch, I soon realized that a whole train would be following me down Old Grove Road. For the first time since the school year began, I wished I was one of the first kids off of the bus. Then I could go and do this thing before any of them were the wiser. Yet, I wasn't. And I would have to deal with them all.

This time on the ride home, Nathan didn't *ask* to sit with me, he just flopped down on the brown material and propped his backpack up in his lap. I was so filled with nerves over what was to come that I just looked at him once and stared out the window again. We didn't talk. In a way, after my announcement this morning, I knew we were in this 'witch' ordeal together. Until I was standing in front of her door, that is. Then I would be completely on my own.

Oh well. I had to suck it up. This was my stupid mess. Me and my Ryder Pride, as my mother called it. Poor old woman. I hoped she'd forgive me. It wasn't like I had asked all these kids to follow me to her garden gate. This was going to be bad, I just knew it.

I was still fretting when I got off the bus. Marching up the walkway, I only paused to throw my backpack in the cupboard under the stairs. Then I walked into the kitchen and told my mother that I was going to ride my bike with a few kids from school. It took some manipulating—it was supposed to rain, after all—but I finally talked her into letting me go.

As I was leaving, she handed me a five dollar bill. In case I wanted to stop anywhere and get a drink or something. I thanked her and headed out to get my bike from the shed. Suddenly, I knew exactly what I was going to do with the money. Pedaling as fast as I could, I headed for the local market.

After making my purchase, I headed toward Old Grove Road with a heavy conscience. Nearing it, I was astonished at the number of kids on bikes and afoot. I knew that my dare had made it around my grade, but *seriously*? Half my grade—if not all of it—was crowded around the rickety sign, or standing next to the apple tree with its rotting perfume. Others were just strung along the road, making a full-blown roadblock of human bodies.

This is ridiculous.

Squaring my little shoulders, I made the decision not to talk to them. If they could gawk at something so un-funny, then I would not give them the time of day. Instead, I pedaled right past them. I could feel them following even before I heard them. The wheels of a bunch of bikes sank into the wet dirt road. A few of the sounds tapered off as some people couldn't get their bikes to plow through the sand-like substance. Luckily, I didn't have to stop. I didn't even have to bother pedaling too hard. Guess that's what happens when your dad's an athletic fiend and gets the really expensive bike for Christmas.

Finally, I made it the mile and a half down to where the old woman's cottage was hiding in the trees. The smell of mint down the road disappeared in the wafting perfume of her garden. Roses, lilacs, basil, mint, rosemary, and thyme. Those were just what I could see over top of her gate. There were a thousand other things I could not identify, but knew that their fragrances were adding to whatever I was smelling.

I stopped at the gate. I'm not totally sure why I was waiting for all of these brats. But I was. Probably because it was their fault that I was here. And they'd all come to gawk at 'the witch' of Old Grove Road. I was all for teaching them a lesson on cowardice and spite. Poor old woman.

I felt bad for bringing this all to her doorstep. But better that I expel the rumors now, while she still lived, than her having to live with them up until her dying day, right?

Sighing, I got off my bike and led it to the fence guarding her property. Knowing that the kickstand would only sink into the soft soil, I just leaned it against the horizontal wooden boards. Here, other forms of climbers slid over and entwined the aged fence, making it appear more green than brown. Bracing myself, I turned to face all of the kids. More were still walking down the road. Apparently they weren't up for walking a whole mile without stopping at least once. I didn't wait for them.

"Go on, Alex. Go and get your proof," Mark taunted.

The cry was taken up in low tones by everyone around. Me, they wanted to confront the witch. But heaven forbid any of them draw her ire unto themselves.

My hands clenched into fists and I walked toward the gate. I was almost surprised to find that Nathan had placed his bike beside mine and walked calmly beside me to the gate.

Almost, but not quite.

Pushing open the gate, I looked down to see that our scuffmarks were still in the salt, though a thin line now covered it. I gripped my tiny paper bag even more tightly, glad I'd thought to bring it. Just as before, I stepped over the white line. Nathan stayed behind me and I smiled slightly at him. Maybe I wasn't a total friendless loser in this place. Not that that bothered me, considering the prospects.

I looked back at all the surprised people behind me. All of them had open mouths and most of the girls had both hands covering theirs. Only Amy didn't react. Mark still looked like he might pee himself. And Becky looked somewhat guilty. Nathan just looked worried. With a last look at all of the kids, I slowly and deliberately closed the gate behind me. I heard a collective gasp.

Turning my back on the spectators, I headed slowly for the pretty arched doorway. A ridiculous image of Hansel and Gretel popped into my head and I shook my head to clear it. As I did so, I realized that I had not yet seen a single cat. My hands balled into fists again and I resisted the urge to glare back at the group.

Stupid brats! Even the cats won't come out while they're around. It was the harshest thing I'd thought of anyone since coming to Cedar Creek. But I meant every word.

It was one thing for an old woman not to stir from her home and have the kids call her a witch. It was quite another when even her animals didn't dare hang around. (I didn't like thinking the cats were afraid of them. But maybe they were.)

Once I regained control of my anger, I marched determinedly toward the door. Ignoring everything in the garden, especially the stone bench, I lifted my little hand and stopped. This was it.

Time to face the music, Lex.

I took a deep breath and...

Chapter Twelve

EXPECTED

The door slowly swung open.

My mouth dropped and my head tilted back to look up at the woman before me. My first thought was, *No way is she a witch.* She wasn't dressed in the long black cloak I had unconsciously expected. (Not from the kids, but from the stone carving of the old woman on the bench. Guess the image stuck with me.)

Her long, light hair hung down in front of her shoulders, like the other woman of stone, trailing all the way to her waist. It wasn't gray, like most elderly women's hair. Rather, it was a real pale white. Almost like sun-dyed blond hair. It could have happened while she was working in the garden or resting on the bench. This must have been the case. It just had to be. Because *no way* did that hair turn white on its own like that. It would have belonged to a much, *much* older woman.

Honestly, she wasn't all that *young* either. But she didn't look nearly as old as the kids made her sound. She was maybe sixty. And that was stretching it, for me. Because her face really wasn't lined or wrinkly. Just a few crow's feet around the eyes. Real faint laugh lines etched around her mouth. And a slight sinking in of the cheeks that marked her for having once been a younger and more vibrant being. She didn't look like a witch.

It seemed like I'd been standing on her door-step for an hour, my mouth hanging open like an idiot, and my hand still in the air as though I was going to knock on her door. Slowly, ever so slowly, I withdrew my upraised hand and clutched the brown paper bag in front of me. Somehow, I remembered how to work my mouth.

Just as I was about to speak, her icy blue eyes landed on my face. I heard my mouth shut with a snap. The eyes slid away to look toward the road and I heard the kids scattering to get out of her line of sight. Still, I knew they wouldn't be going far. The woman looked back at me, her eyes filled with a distant knowledge. I felt weak, small, and helpless as I stood at her mercy. Not because part of me still wondered if she were a witch, but because a big part of me wondered if she was going to call my parents.

"Come. I've been expecting you."

My mouth fell open again as she stepped aside and opened the door wider. I couldn't take my eyes from her face. Not even to sneak a peek into her home—which I was extremely curious about. For a long time, I stood there, unable to believe what she had just said.

Suddenly, I heard a meow from inside. My eyes broke from hers to land on the black cat who had led me to this inevitable destination. Jade eyes stared coldly at me. But the cold was one of understanding and knowledge. Things I had always felt comfortable with. As I did now. Without taking my eyes off the familiar feline, I stepped over the threshold and was soon in the woman's house.

Behind me, the door closed with a significant thud. My heartbeat picked up the pace as I suddenly realized what I'd done. If my parents could see me now... A shiver ran up my spine. My legs started to shake and I locked my knees in order to stay upright.

In order to distract myself from my fear, I let my eyes roam over her home. It looked like the house had only two other rooms besides the one I was in. The main room served as kitchen, dining room, and living area. I supposed that the small, walled off corner with two doors led to her bedroom and bathroom.

As I took in details, I found myself to be a little smug. A gas-lighting stove rested in the kitchen next to the minuscule counter space. The refrigerator was old, and had a slightly rounded appearance toward the top. Most of the kitchen was taken up by a large, wooden plank table. It was at least four inches thick and made of age-darkened cedar, I think. Four matching chairs rested around it, though one was shoved a little to the side.

Underneath the table sat six cats. Two were black as pitch. Not a speck of white on them. The tuxedo cat and tabby sat side by side. One cat, the ashy gray, barely looked at me as it cleaned its paw. The last was a gray with deep black markings like tattoos across its slinky body.

My eyes drifted away from the cats to the fireplace nearby. There was an ancient metal grate across it, keeping a majority of the sparks from hitting something flammable. Strangely, the smell of the burning wood and sound of the crackling fire was more comforting than it was frightening.

Especially after that horrible night where the fire was just a vision of orange, dancing flames. No sound or smell to let me know if it was real or not. It was ghost fire. Just like that little girl.

As if thinking about it would make something materialize from just that situation, my eyes suddenly trailed across the room to find an old, wooden rocking chair. Just looking at it, I could hear the creaks of the one in my delusion—for lack of a better word. I almost lost my footing right then. In my head, she was right there, staring at her hands, auburn curls hanging around her shoulders. I shook my head hurriedly, eager to escape the image.

"What is your name child?"

I jumped on hearing the old woman's voice and turned my head to watch her with wide eyes as she drifted past me. "A-A-Alexandria," I finally gasped out.

The woman turned to study me. In the much dimmer light, she didn't look as young or unthreatening as she had out in the sunshine. Her face was twisted into a studying look as her eyes grazed my figure.

"How old are you, Alexandria?"

I gulped and tried to answer with a clear voice. "Nine."

The woman's eyes widened but she said nothing on the matter.

As she stood there, studying me with one finger over her lips, her other hand tucked beneath her elbow, my fear began to recede. Curiosity took its place.

"Were you really expecting me? Or did you just say that?" I blurted out. A faint smile touched her lips before being wiped away.

"Yes, I was expecting you. I will not tell you something I do not mean. Dishonesty is not welcome in this house." Beneath the table, all of the cats shifted except the two black ones.

"Why were you expecting me?"

"I pulled down an extra plate." She could see that I was confused and she shifted so that I could see two dinner plates setting on the table. I still didn't get it and she smiled to herself once more. "There is an old superstition: to have too many plates on a table means guests. Another says that that guest will come hungry. Is this true?"

Until she said that, food had been far from my mind. But I'd missed my afternoon snack in my hurry to get my dare over with. Before I had a chance to answer, my stomach growled loud enough for her to plainly hear. Another smile and she turned toward the counter. Taking from a bowl of fruit, she pulled out a bright red apple.

I'd moved without thought again. One moment I was standing just inside the door, the next I was leaning against the side of the table. From the other side, she handed the apple to me. Snow White entered my head and I could do nothing but stare at it.

"Are you really a witch?" The words were out of my mouth before I could think. As soon as I said them, my eyes shot to the floor as my face heated with a blush. When I finally did get the courage to look up, I saw that her mouth was turned up into a small smile. Her eyes, however, were cold with knowledge. She intimidated me.

"Well, Alexandria, what do you think?"

Chapter Thirteen

MORGAN LE FAY

The words came out almost milky, smooth and thicker than water with their texture. Her tone almost had a mocking to it, but her eyes were serious. She honestly wanted to know what I thought. It forced me to think about the question carefully.

I had to take in the evidence. So far, nothing was conclusive. Just a number of cats and a stone bench with my face carved in it. Salt lines and gargoyles, as well. And an uncanny ability to know when she'll receive nosy visitors. But that wasn't enough to call her a witch. Was it?

"I don't know."

Slowly, she pulled out the chair on her side of the table and sat down. I mimicked her just as slowly, placing the apple on the table between us.

"Why not? What do you think of when you hear the word 'witch'?"

"Fairy tales," I admitted, the list of evil witches marching through my head.

"Oh? And I am not like them?" her voice said with a laugh. I smiled shyly.

"*Are* you a witch like them? Like the evil queen in 'Snow White'? Or like Morgan le Fay?" My confidence grew with each word. But it faded as soon as her icy eyes pierced into mine. For a minute, she was silent.

"Like your evil queen, no. But I do admit to taking after your Morgan le Fay."

For a minute I was stunned. Did she really just admit to being a witch? A *real* witch? Those kids weren't making this up? My mind couldn't fully handle that and I felt myself shoot up-wards. The cats in the area, already scattered from when we sat down, now began to hiss from various perches around the house. Blood rushed in my ears and the room spun.

"Are ... are you really a witch like Morgan le Fay?" I stammered. She didn't answer until the room had stopped spinning. I had to grip the back of my chair for support while my legs shook.

"I am." Calm. How could she admit such a thing and be sitting there so calmly? My head spun. "For Goddess's sake child, sit down." I did as she commanded, my quaking legs giving me no other options.

"Goddess?" I asked, holding my head in my hands. I heard her sigh.

"My, my, you have a lot to learn, my dear." Suddenly, the ashy gray cat gave a hiss and pawed at the window. The witch's eyes shot up to stare at him knowingly before turning back to me. "Best to wait for another time. Come. It's time for you to head home."

I didn't question her judgment. The other kids probably all thought I was Alex-stew right about now. My irritation also came back full force when I realized that the cats really were being cooped up because of them. I stood up and turned toward the door. It wasn't until I had my hand on the handle that I remembered the garden gate and the ruined salt line. Shame came over me and I walked slowly back to the table.

"I forgot to give you this," I muttered, reaching into the brown paper bag and pulling out a container of sea salt. "My mom always says sea salt is better for you than regular. I'm sorry I ruined your line Tuesday."

The witch smiled a real smile at me this time. "Thank you, Alexandria. I will wait to see if you brave another visit. Now that you have an idea of what I am."

The challenge there, I grinned widely, unable to help myself. "Oh, I'll be back," I assured her in a plucky tone. In the same instant, I snatched the red apple up off the table and headed back toward the door. Once more, I stopped. Looking back over my shoulder, I asked, "What's your name?"

A golden laugh filled the air. "Call me Morgan, my dear Alexandria. Call me Morgan," she added again in subdued seriousness. I nodded solemnly, still smiling. Then another question puckered my brow.

"Do you want me to tell *them* that you're a witch?"

"I brook no dishonesty in my house. I would not ask for a lie from your lips."

My brow cleared and I smiled brightly.

"Goodbye, Morgan. I'll see you," I said and finally left the stone cottage.

For the first time since moving to Cedar Creek, I didn't feel alone. Not really. I mean, since moving here I'd experienced some really crazy stuff. Somehow I knew that Morgan had, too. And maybe, *just maybe,* she could help me through my craziness. Preferably before I ended up in a straitjacket and padded room. Maybe Morgan was a step toward the mysterious little girl and her appearances. I hoped so.

As I walked up the path to the garden gate, I noticed the heads peeking from around bushes and others who stood only a few feet from the gate. I smiled as I continued along. At the gate stood Nathan, and he pushed it open on my approach. Nodding my thanks, I stepped carefully over the salt line before closing the gate behind me.

Without saying one word, I headed for my bike. By now, there were a bunch of kids crowding the road. Every single one of them stared at me with wide eyes. Again, most of their mouths hung open.

Ignoring them, I pulled my bike away from

the fence and faced it toward Norfolk Street. I mentally counted down from five before someone finally managed to say my name. Turning back with a polite expression, I could see Becky's mouth working to say something. I waited patiently.

"Well?" she finally demanded.

Being a little dramatic, I rolled my right shoulder in a shrug and smiled just slightly. "She's a witch," I announced, and then I took a bite of the bright red apple Morgan had given to me.

Before they could recover, I stood up on my bike and pedaled my way home.

Chapter Fourteen

RANDOM KEYS

I ate every bite of that apple on the way home, riding one-handed most of the time. And all the while, I was giggling. Their faces were amazing. My Ryder Pride was on a bright and fluffy cloud high up in the air. Nothing could touch it. When I got home, my mother must have thought I was a nightmare to deal with, what with me prancing around in such a good mood.

So free, I was feeling, that I even dared to head for the piano. Not caring that I didn't know how to play, I placed my fingers as I had seen girls do on TV and started to play. I hit whatever sounded good. Only when the last, lonely note hung in the air did I realize why my tune had sounded famil-iar. Before I had time to contemplate it, I heard clapping in the corner of the room. I whipped around to see my mother smiling at me in the doorway. My face burned with a scarlet blush.

"Are you sure you need lessons? You seem to know how to play already." I knew that look. She was thinking I was some sort of prodigy. In truth, my hands had just been possessed. And I hadn't even realized it.

"I was just pressing random keys. I have no idea what I'm doing," I answered honestly. My mother smiled slyly as she crossed the room to sit beside me.

"*This* is hitting random keys," she said and began prancing her fingers along the ivory. I laughed, taking my fingers along with hers but on the deeper end of the piano. Together, we played and laughed.

Finally, we left the instrument. She went to make dinner. I went to retrieve my backpack and carried it up to my room. I didn't have homework, so I just left it next to my desk. Then I turned to head back downstairs, with only a glance around my room.

I trudged down the stairs. Most of my good mood had evaporated with the piano playing. It wasn't me who was playing that haunted melody. I knew that much to be true.

Absently, I wondered if I would hear the piano again tonight. Would she feel the need to prove that she was better, even as a ghost, than she was when using me?

She used me! I shivered, stopping at the bottom of the stairs. Glancing into the parlor, I shivered again.

All growing up, I'd heard all kinds of ghost stories. Not that I'd given any merit to kids' tales. Time after time, a kid would claim seeing a spirit or hearing strange noises, like talking, in the middle of the night. But that's all it ever was. A glimpse. A whisper. Never more than that.

Going on this evidence, it scared me even more. Because it meant that this ghost, this girl, was even stronger than the ghosts that kids from across the country had told me about. She physically played the piano—by herself—with only her ghostly fingers. Then she made flames appear from nothing. She'd sat for a long time in a rocking chair that had not been in the room before. And then she'd used me, and I didn't even realize it.

Instead of heading toward the kitchen and trying to pretend cheerfulness in front of my mother, I turned around and headed right back up to my room. I couldn't face her while I was still reeling. What did that girl *do* to me? What did she want? *Why me?*

For a minute, I just stood inside the doorway to my room, looking over every detail. No fire. No ghostly rocking chair. No little girl. I sighed in relief, though I knew it was too early to celebrate. She was a nocturnal hunter, attacking only at night when I was most vulnerable. Shivering again, I moved farther into the room.

Glancing at my bookshelf, I thought about reading one of the many volumes. But I wasn't in the mood to read. I wasn't in the mood to do anything. Turning to my northern window, I pulled aside the filmy white curtain and opened the casement. A light breeze carried in the smell of rain and flowers. I closed my eyes and leaned my head out. My long hair was pulled out and got tangled in the ivy. Giggling, I didn't open my eyes.

"Lexi Girl, what do you think you're doing?" I heard my dad call.

My eyes snapped open and I looked down into his hard expression. Biting my lip, I realized that I had been leaning quite a ways out of the window and this had obviously frightened him. I quickly called down an apology and pulled back inside. One stubborn strand of hair refused to relinquish its grasp on the ivy vine. Finally, with a last tug, I brought tangled hair and an ivy leaf inside. With a smile, I pulled the ivy from my hair and held it up to my nose. The fresh smell rolled off of it and filled my nostrils before I turned and set it on my desk. Once I'd closed the window, I hurriedly ran down to greet my father and renew my apology.

Dinner didn't last long, like usual, and I was soon back in my bedroom. I didn't have the heart to be hanging around my parents tonight. Best that I get really acquainted with my room before the little girl found her way back up here.

I soon found myself at my desk. The book my dad had given me still sat there, unopened. My captured ivy leaf still had a bit of stem to it and I lifted it into the air, just to watch it float back down to the desktop again.

"Hey baby, time for bed," my mom said as she

knocked on my door, opening it inch by inch. For the first time, I looked at my alarm clock. Sure enough, my bedtime was upon me.

My mom tucked me in and when she asked if I'd like her to stay, I bravely said no and let her leave. Of course, as soon as she closed the door, I was regretting it. I had never been one of those kids who admitted to being afraid of the dark. And after a few years, I no longer was. But as I lay there in the black room, my eyes taking forever to adjust, I couldn't help my increasing heartbeat.

Just leave me alone. For one more night. Just leave me alone, I prayed silently. I chanted this mantra in my head over and over again.

I woke up to my alarm clock crying out at me. Rolling over in a swift motion, my hand shot out and turned off the alarm. Sitting up in bed took a little bit longer. I laid back and stared at the white, filmy fabric of my canopy and studied the translucent folds and shadows of it.

She left me alone, I thought with a smile. There had been no music or flashing orange lights all night long. I felt giddy with relief. At the same time, I knew that she wouldn't give me a pass this weekend. Yet, the fact that it was Friday made it all that more refreshing. I could deal with her on my own time this weekend.

Without wasting a minute longer, I jumped out of bed and went to get ready for school. Once I was clean and dressed, I came back into my bedroom to grab my backpack. Just as I was turning to leave, I noticed something very strange.

The book my father had given me was wide open on the desk. And a single ivy leaf rested on top of a black and white photo. Just as I was about to have a look, my mother called from downstairs. With a sigh, I turned and headed for her voice. I would just have to investigate after school.

Chapter Fifteen

OPEN BOOK

For the first time in my young life, I was faced with one of those really long, awkward pauses that comes from one's sudden appearance. At least, that's what happened the second I got on the bus that morning. And each time someone else got on, they would stare at me for a minute before whispers were being traded behind little hands. All the while, they kept looking at me.

I did my best to ignore them, but it was difficult. Nathan sat with me again that morning. This time, I was grateful. Our bus could get pretty crowded and I didn't want to sit with someone who would only gawk at me. Somehow, Nathan and I were well on our way to having one of those strange always-silent-but-stuck-together friendships.

As the ride wore on, I began to recognize more and more of the faces that stared at me. I'd seen them on Old Grove Road yesterday afternoon. Each one angered me and I did my best to just stare out the window. Right then I swore that I wouldn't tell them any more about what had happened. I would just keep silent, no matter what they said or did to try and get my attention.

Besides, it wasn't like I didn't have other things to worry about. *What's in that book?* I thought yet again. My mind trailed back to ivy leaves and hidden photographs. It would have been easier if I had someone to talk to about it. But Nathan wasn't an option.

As the bus stopped at the school, all of us stood and lined up in the aisle in order to get off. I was separated from everyone else by a wide margin as they continued to stare. Only Nathan treated me normally. Probably because everyone was treating him almost as abnormally as me. Oh yeah, we were stuck together now.

Most of my school day went on as a normal Cedar Creek Elementary day would for me. That is to say: I got questioned in every class. There were strange people trying to talk with me at lunch. And I got swamped at recess. Everyone wanted to know the same thing: What happened in the witch's cottage? True to my oath, I didn't say a word. I just glared frostily at them and walked away.

I was actually quite proud of myself. Having issues with backing down, it proved hard when people started calling me a baby and other mean things. But I knew that they were just trying to goad me into telling them something. Unfortunately for them, I knew what self-discipline meant. And I would not break under some ridiculous taunts.

Finally, however, my Friday school day was over. And all I had for homework was a reading assignment and an order to study for my math test on Monday.

As I got off the bus, my stomach was filled with so many butterflies, I wondered if some were going to try to make an escape out of my mouth. Each step felt like it weighed a ton as I walked toward the house. Once I made it through the door, my feet dragged to the closet under the stairs as I began to hang up my coat and kick off my shoes. Leaving my backpack there, I headed for the kitchen to give my mother some of my time before I went upstairs to investigate.

The book was just how I left it this morning. It was open to a page near the end, a large ivy leaf covering the entire black and white photo on the left side of the page. On the right side, in large black letters, it said: ***The Disappearance of Alyssa Rice***.

I knew that the story was going to frighten me. I knew that this would be the mystery surrounding my ghost girl. Of course, I knew that the picture would be of her. There was no need to remove the ivy leaf just to see her there, staring at the camera. No need, but I did anyway.

Gasping, I felt the leaf slip from my fingers, fluttering to the floor beside the desk. It wasn't just *a* picture of Alyssa. It was *the* picture! Maybe she was sitting on a piano bench rather than in a rocking chair, but the position was just alike. Her little white ankles crossed, the dress flowing over her knees. And her hands, pearly white, clasped together. The curls had a shine from some lighting, but I knew that they were auburn in color and looked like copper in firelight. Now, the only difference was that she stared up into the camera. Dark eyes were framed by thick, black lashes and the glow in them was nothing like the flat blackness that had sent me into a fainting spell. Again, I shivered.

Underneath the large photo, the caption read: *Alyssa Rice, 9, sitting at the Grand Piano, 9 March 1922. Photograph provided by Cedar Creek Academy of Musical Arts.*

For a long minute, I just stared at the girl in the picture. The dress was exactly the same. I knew that this was the night she'd died. And for the first time, I thought of her as Alyssa the person, not the ghost. Shame filled me as I looked down at this little girl who had lost her life so long ago.

Finally, I turned to the next page. The story of Alyssa Rice was even sadder than I expected.

Chapter Sixteen

ALYSSA RICE

Alyssa Mae Rice was born on May 12, 1912 to Mr. Peter Rice and Mrs. Mary Rice. From her deeply copper curls, her infectious smile, and charming personality, this was one girl who amazed the world.

From infancy, Alyssa was brought up to admire music. At only a month old, her mother had taken her to her first concert at the Cedar Creek Academy of Musical Arts auditorium. It was their tenth annual concert celebrating the induction of the school. Without the Rice family, the Academy would not have made it through their first year. Now, there was a new little Rice to appreciate the impressive performances the Academy had to offer.

After growing up in the halls of the Academy, young Alyssa soon became a rising star and an example to all who knew her. At the tender age of four, she was learning to play both the piano and the harp. With nimble fingers and steadiness of character, Alyssa soon became Cedar Creek's own musical prodigy.

Five more years would follow this child through her glorious rise. The piano had claimed her interest and no one could doubt that she was gifted with the ivory. Mr. and Mrs. Rice, instead of sending her to school, chose to hire private tutors so that she would be able to learn where she was most comfortable.

During that fateful week in March, Alyssa's young life had reached a peak.

A national competition had been held for musicians of all ages. Narrowing down a winner had taken weeks upon weeks for the fretting judges. Finally, the finalists had been announced. Alyssa Rice, age 9, had been at the top of the list.

March 9, 1922 would bring about one of the greatest victories Alyssa was ever to receive. It would also be the most tragic day the Rice family was ever forced to live through.

During a party to celebrate her many accomplishments, young Alyssa was glowing with pride, witnesses claimed. She danced through the crowd in the same gold and ivory dress she had worn during the concert that *had decided her victory. Ringlets of her auburn hair were held back by a hairpiece made of golden roses. Alyssa was said to pose at her beloved piano for an hour to accommodate her parents and guests.*

In a house so filled with admirers--all come to praise such a wonderful young musician--one would think Alyssa could not have turned around without someone noticing. And yet, this beautiful, intelligent child had been missing for upwards of an hour before her mother finally noticed her disappearance. Screaming her loss, a distraught Mrs. Rice was said to have fainted when it was known that, after a lengthy search of the house, Alyssa was nowhere to be found.

The police were called immediately to the Rice household. Every detail was gone over again and again. All of the visitors of that night, even those who had left early, were questioned extensively about the disappearance of Cedar Creek's most valuable treasure. Yet, they each came back empty-handed.

For days the police searched for any clue. The Rice family waited for a ransom letter or demand from kidnappers. Alyssa's disappearance was advertised everywhere as they searched for the young girl. Nothing was ever found.

Years would come to pass. With Alyssa's disap-

pearance keeping Cedar Creek on its toes, other things were lost. Including the Cedar Creek Academy of Musical Arts. And after a decade without finding Alyssa, the Rice family was finally forced to admit that they would never see their crown jewel again. Mr. and Mrs. Rice left Cedar Creek on the day of Alyssa's twentieth birthday. They took nothing with them.

To this very day, people who pass by the house on Verity Lane wonder what happened to the girl with the auburn curls and skill with the ivory keys. As they stare at the windows of the red brick house, they ask themselves how a child could vanish from a party thrown in her honor. It makes them ponder over how a child so beloved could have disappeared so suddenly, without a trace to be found. Then they wonder if something like what happened to Alyssa Rice could happen to their own child.

Chills run up their spines and their eyes automatically follow the ivy vines as they reach for the sky. A breeze willfully shakes the leaves of the green plants, doused with splashes of red, and their eyes travel to the far right window on the second story. There will their eyes pause and they might believe they were imagining things. For only a moment, a girl with pearly white skin and copper ringlets will be seen, standing in the window. One blink later, and she is gone. Just like the first time she had disappeared.

"Music is the way I share my heart with the world." - Alyssa Rice

Chapter Seventeen

LONELY

I shivered as I read the last words. It was so sad. Alyssa had been a good, sweet, kind girl. A musical prodigy. And in one night, one single moment, Alyssa had disappeared. They never found anything to tell them what happened to her. Then, when her parents finally gave up, they just left everything behind. Like she wasn't worth remembering. As if they didn't *want* to remember their daughter.

My eyes filled with tears and I scrubbed them away with the back of my hand. I couldn't imagine not being cared about. Not being wanted enough that you'd just let a stranger keep everything. Every memory, everything she'd touched, every object she'd coveted and cherished. They had taken nothing with them. Just as if they wanted her to fade from existence. Again, I felt myself begin to cry.

I slammed the book closed and jumped up and ran into the bathroom. While I was in there, I took a shower, hoping that the hot water would pound the image of Alyssa sitting on the piano bench out of my head. I tried to find something else to see other than her dark eyes, tumbling curls, and that bland expression. It was this expression that made me suddenly hurry from the shower. Though I couldn't have forgotten a single detail about the photograph, I was still in a hurry to double-check.

With my hair dripping out a path behind me on the smooth wood floor, I walked swiftly to my desk. It took a while of searching the book, but I finally found the picture of Alyssa. I was right. In no way was this little girl happy. No matter if she had won some major competition, she was not excited or proud, as the story suggested. There was no glow of life in her skin. Her features were utterly blank. Refusing to display any form of emotion, good or bad. But in her eyes, I could see something. Loneliness.

Alyssa was lonely. Alive or dead.

There had to be a reason for it. Every time I turned around, Alyssa was showing me something new and different. She wanted me to see her pose, to see the empty rocking chair, and the fire in the fireplace. And she most definitely wanted me to read her story. The story of what happened to her that night. Alyssa had even given me a gift; an ivy leaf that I now picked up off the floor.

Suddenly, there was a light knock on my bedroom door. Hurriedly, I put the leaf in the book and slammed it closed, whipping about to face the door. My mother was just poking her head in, an apologetic smile on her face. My heart had been racing and I was working to slow it.

"Hey baby. Your father called. He won't be home for dinner. What do you say to pizza and a movie?" I was barely able to smile as I nodded my head.

"Sure. Sounds great," I told her. She smiled and said she'd order our favorite before backing out of the room. I let out a big sigh.

Looking at my clock, I realized that I had

only been upstairs for an hour and a half. It seemed so much longer. I felt like it should be dark already, but the sun was still out, proving me wrong. Trying to shake all thought of Alyssa's story out of my head, I placed the book on the bookshelf and headed downstairs to have dinner with my mom.

That night, I waited for Alyssa. I waited for her to show me something. To give me some clue as to what might have happened to her. For hours I sat up waiting. Nothing happened. When I went to bed, I slept with the expectation of being woken. Still nothing. And when I woke up with no sign of my ghostly companion, I made a decision.

I would go looking for her.

Chapter Eighteen

SEARCHING

Okay, my chances of finding her...? Realistically? Not good. After all, people had been searching for Alyssa for decades. No one's seen her since that night she disappeared. Still, she contacted me. She wanted me to know these things for a reason. Who had a better chance of finding Ghost Alyssa? It wasn't like I was looking for her body. (Well, not yet, anyway. Someday I would have to give that a shot. To put her to rest. But first things first...)

After I got dressed, I began a thorough investigation of the house. Obviously, I started with my bedroom, where the most activity was. I looked under the bed and checked every drawer of the desk. Even the bookshelf got searched time and again. I found nothing, unfortunately. Double-checking everything once more, I finally gave up and proceeded to search the rest of the house.

I ended up in the parlor. It was the logical next move. Alyssa's piano stood there, a silent testament of her last night in the house. Possibly the only witness as to what really happened to her. That thought made me nervous as I slowly approached it.

The first thing I did was look at all of the keys, thinking maybe something would be stuck between them. Then I turned to the bench and levered the top open. All I found in there was sheet music. Mozart. Beethoven. Bach. And many others. Sighing, I put the cushioned seat down and turned back to the actual instrument. I was just trying to lift the heavy back of the piano when my mom came in.

"Lex? What are you doing?"

I didn't have time to come up with a clever lie that she would actually believe. Besides that, I hated liars. So I told her part of the truth.

"I'm trying to lift this. I want to see what's inside," I answered, pushing on the lid experimentally as though to give her an example. Mom rolled her eyes and strode over to help me.

"And why are we doing this?" she questioned. I shrugged, trying to look innocent and casual about the whole thing. All the while, however, my heart was racing, wondering if anything might actually be inside.

When we finally got it open, I stuck my head into the space. Mom kept shooting me worried glances, and held the lid securely away from my head. I had to stop myself from expelling a disappointed sigh. There was nothing—*Wait! What was that?*

Something was glittering in the sunlight that poured in from the nearby window. I eased my arm in and attempted to pull out the glittering object but I couldn't reach it. And there was *no way* that I was going to ask my mom to pull it out for me.

"Alexandria Marie! What are you doing?" my mother snapped and I hurriedly pulled my arm out and stepped back. She gently lowered the lid, officially closing off whatever chance I had in pulling out the shiny object. My heart sank in my chest.

"I just wanted to see something," I told her

in a chagrinned tone. At first she was angry, but after taking one look at my face, she sighed and shook her head.

"Hey, baby, it's okay. You just scared me for a second there." I bowed my head in shame, causing my mother to lift my chin and kiss my forehead. "I almost forgot why I came looking for you."

"What? Why?"

"I asked around and, yesterday afternoon, Mrs. Hodge finally told me that there is a local piano teacher. Her name is Catherine Herring. I was told that she has a studio in town. We can sign you up today, if you like?"

I was instantly torn. On one hand, it was just signing up right? On the other, Alyssa was still missing. Which was more important? Finally, I decided to go with my mom and sign up. I could search when we came back. Besides, if Alyssa needed my help all that badly, she'd let me know. And what was more important than *not* making my parents suspicious? Even Alyssa would understand that.

As we were getting into my mom's sedan, I couldn't stop myself from looking up at my bedroom window. For one whole second, I thought

I saw the curtains flutter. *I'll be right back,* I thought to the ghost in my room. *At least I know she's still around,* I added to myself. Stifling a sigh, I got into the car and my mom pulled out of the driveway.

Just as I had predicted, it did not take us long to sign up. Together, my mother and I decided that Thursday afternoons would be best for my lessons. That way it didn't cut into my weekend. Plus, Catherine only had two days left open that weren't completely jam-packed with students and other plans. So, after all this was over, I was soon standing in my room once more.

After another brief search, I realized that Alyssa was gone again. She certainly wasn't going to be easy to find. With a sigh, I turned and began to search rooms I was sure she wasn't in, just to cross them off the list. The bathrooms I checked, all of the closets I could get to, and the kitchen. Living room and spare bedrooms were looked through. As was the office. Nothing.

I was almost sure that she was in my room. Either that or the parlor. I couldn't see where else she could possibly be. Except, of course, in the yard. Having just thought of it, I was soon tying shoes on my feet and headed out to the shed where my bike was kept and to the garage that had also been an addition on the property. Nothing in either of them.

Strolling through the backyard, I took a deep breath of the fragrant air. My body was already warming to the intense sunshine and I closed my eyes and stood still, letting the heat soak into my pale skin. After a minute, I looked up.

There, on the other side of the garage, was something I had not truly noticed before. Obviously I had known about the giant oak that towered above the garage and sat on the edge of our backyard. What I hadn't noticed was the plain, simply made swing that hung from its branches. It was just a wide board drilled with holes that had rope long-ago grown into the tree.

Without thinking about it, I strode to the swing and sat down. I pushed off and swung my legs appropriately, gaining momentum as I worked my body with the swing. In no time at all, I had forgotten everything. I'd forgotten why the swing was mysterious. I had no thoughts as to the garden filled with plants that I had no names for. My thoughts did not drift over the parlor or my bedroom. In that whole block of time, my only focus was on my legs, moving back and forth time and again.

I only stopped when I happened to glance up and see Alyssa.

My feet immediately dragged the ground, digging in the dirt tracks many feet had taken over time. I dared not to take my eyes from her. Every time I did, I risked the chance of not seeing her again. Now, she looked down at me from the third floor window. Only two windows looked down from the third floor, one at the front of the house and one at the back, since that was considered the attic by the family that was here before us.

So, that's where you're hiding, I thought to my ghostly counterpart. Slowly, I stood up and headed for the back door. Just before I lost sight of her, she turned from the window and disappeared. She was waiting for me.

I entered the backdoor into the kitchen and kicked off my shoes. Mom was in the office, grading papers. This made me smile and I picked up my shoes and ran upstairs to throw them in my bedroom. Once this was done, I searched the common hallway doors, looking for the one that held the stairs that led to the attic.

As I was going down the hall, I reached one door and began to pull on the handle, expecting it to yield easily. It didn't. Again and again I tried the knob, only to do so in vain. The door was locked. And the only way I knew that it was the door I searched for was by looking through the keyhole. I prayed that Alyssa had had enough of frightening me; else, it would be a great opportunity to scare the wits out of me when I put my eye to that keyhole. Sighing, I did it anyway.

Yes. The door was hiding stairs leading to the attic. And setting on the stairs, right at eye level, was a pretty little snow globe. In the gloom, I couldn't make out what was inside of the globe. A gut feeling told me that it would be this house, though. The large brick building with a crown of chimneys and ivy climbing the sides. Even though I couldn't see it, I knew.

I tried the door one last time. Again, it did not yield. Sighing, I trudged back to my room, my entire being filled with frustration. For now, my Alyssa Rice mystery was put on an indefinite hold.

Chapter Nineteen

MEDITATING

I couldn't stay in the house after my failure. Even if it meant I'd see Alyssa in my room again or something else. The frustration was just too much for me and I still had a whole day to kill. After explaining my boredom to my mother, I headed for the shed.

Pulling my bike out, I shot a last glance at the attic window. Nothing. I sighed and stood up on the pedals, directing the bike up the driveway. I lost my thoughts in the movement of my legs and feet pushing on the pedals. My body took me to my destination before I'd even realized I wanted to go there. Though I should have suspected something like this would occur.

Before I knew it, I had parked my bike and

leaned it against the old, wooden fence. Then I stepped carefully around to the path and patted one of the gargoyles on the head as I swung open the gate. Looking down, I saw the large white crystals of the sea salt I'd brought. A smile broke out on my face as I knew I had been forgiven. Stepping carefully over the line, I entered the witch's garden.

I skipped to the door and reached my little hand up as before. This time, though, the door didn't swing open for me. But I still didn't get a chance to knock.

"Hello, Alexandria," Morgan's voice said.

I whipped around as my heart skipped a beat. She was sitting on the far end of the bench, her long, black skirt covering the carving of the Crone. The Mother was still exposed, as was the Maiden, who stared at me with her cold, stone eyes. I refocused on Morgan eagerly.

"Hello, Morgan," I answered shyly, still trying to get over the fright.

"So you were brave enough to return. You have courage."

I found myself smiling, remembering why I'd agreed to come back. Shaking my head, I said,

"Not courage. Pride. Ryder Pride." I giggled a little at that and Morgan's melodic chuckle filled the air.

"I see. And are you content with this 'Ryder Pride'?" Morgan asked, raising an eyebrow. She motioned me to take a seat and I moved to sit on the Maiden side of the bench. The perfect image of the Mother was left uncovered between us. I refused to look at her. As I sat down, my feline friend jumped up and I began petting her absentmindedly.

"I guess so. I mean, it can get me into some sticky situations. But I'd rather be proud of myself and my accomplishments rather than always being self-conscious."

"That is a responsible answer."

I smiled. "I'm a responsible person."

"So, prideful young Alexandria, what brings you to my home today?"

I bit my lip, unsure how to answer. "I don't know," I told her slowly. "I just needed time away from my own house. My feet led me here."

"Well, there must be some reason you are here."

I shrugged and looked around. The garden

was beautiful, and vibrant with life. Hard to believe, considering how quickly summer would fade and how fast autumn would come to replace it. My eyes trailed over the unfamiliar plants and flowers, wishing I had more knowledge as to what they were. Finally, my eyes strayed back to Morgan.

"What makes you a witch?" I asked before thinking through my question.

"What do you mean?" An indulgent smile pulled at her thin lips as she studied me.

"I mean: How'd you become one? Do you do spells and magic? Why do you claim being a witch?" The words just continued to shoot out of my mouth.

"I was raised a witch. Yes, I do rituals, spells, and a great deal of magick. I claim witchcraft because of my own pride. I shall not hide what I am."

"Do you have a power?" I felt silly asking, but it was one of those questions that come with being nine and not understanding what you're really talking about.

"We all have power," she answered simply. I rolled my eyes.

"I meant a magical power. Like seeing the future or moving objects with your mind or—"

"Seeing the deceased?" Just then, something was lodged in my throat and I couldn't talk. Instead, I nodded, my curiosity reaching a full peak. Morgan nodded as well. "We all have power, Alexandria. It is just more hidden for some people than it is for others. Those who search to uncover their own power find themselves more gifted than they ever thought possible."

I soaked the words in like a sponge. They tumbled around in my head as I tried to make sense of them. "Is it not hidden from you?" I murmured, my mind still miles away.

Morgan smiled and turned to look out over the garden, the sunshine lighting up her face. "Not since I learned to open my mind. And my heart. No. It is no longer hidden from me."

"Can you show me?" I needed proof. It was the way I was raised.

"No," Morgan stated, shaking her head.

My bottom lip automatically pushed out in a pout. "Why not?"

Morgan bent her head just slightly more to look me in the eye.

"I will show you what I can do, when you show me what you can do," she said quietly, her icy eyes twinkling with mischief. I was confused, and a little frightened.

"I can't do anything," I replied in the same whiny voice that came with my pout.

"Then we should do something about that."

It took me a whole minute to realize what she was saying. When I finally got it, my mouth fell open and my eyes widened in shock. I was so surprised that I couldn't even move. Finally, I remembered how to speak.

"You ... you want to make me a witch? Like you? How?"

"I will teach you, if that be your wish. However, you must know that magick is a sacred gift. Not one to be flouted about. The responsibility of a witch is to remain silent. Magick is for you and you alone. To speak of it is to diminish it. Weaken it. Now, Alexandria, are you capable of keeping such a great secret?"

Though I hated to admit it, she had a point. This was not an easy choice to make and I had to think it through. I had to know what it would mean for me to go through with this. What I would be.

"What does it mean to be a witch, Morgan? What will you teach me?"

A look passed over her face then. Her icy eyes seemed to soften and her thin lips pulled into a pleased little smile. As she studied me, I got the sense that I had somehow earned her approval with my questions. Maybe because I'd questioned it in the first place. I was willing to take it as seriously as she wanted me to.

"Alexandria, what is the golden rule they teach you in school?"

Confusion twisted my features before I answered slowly, "Treat others as you would like to be treated."

"'An' it harm none, do as ye will.' It is known as the Wiccan Rede, but the sentiments are far older than the religion itself. And it encompasses all living creatures. From grass to horse, tree to beetle, and flower to human. An' it harm none, do what ye will. It is the law of magick just as it is the law of life. That is what I wish to teach you, Alexandria. That is all I wish to teach." I waited for her to continue, but her eyes were distant, seeing something beyond myself, and I settled back to ponder what she'd just said.

For a long moment, I sat there with my brow furrowed and my teeth stuck in my bottom lip. What to do? The choice was up to me. Morgan wasn't willing to push me either way. And I was used to being pushed. But it was my decision. Did I, or did I not, want to learn magick?

If I learned magick, maybe I could help Alyssa even more. Besides, despite the seriousness, magick sounded really fun.

"I want to learn," I announced.

Morgan's eyes snapped back to this place and time in order to fully study me. "You are sure? Magick is not something to trifle with, Alexandria. It requires hard work, attention to detail, and much self-discipline."

"Yes, I'm sure. I was practically raised for this," I added the last with a smile.

"Then we will start with something basic, but very rewarding," she replied.

"What?"

A sly smile formed on her pink lips. "Meditating."

"Meditating?" I asked incredulously.

"Yes." I tried to hide my disappointment.

I was hoping we'd start with something more magickal. "You can't practice magick if you can't focus your mind properly. Otherwise, things could work into the magick you did not expect, and certainly did not wish for."

I nodded at her explanation, sighing in defeat.

"So, how do I meditate? Do I have to sit like this?" I asked, moving into the position I'd seen on TV. Morgan laughed and shook her head.

"No. You want to be comfortable. But I don't suggest trying it in a bed. That is most often too comfortable," she added with a small chuckle. I nodded, taking mental notes. "I often sit right here to meditate. The fresh air does good to your lungs, as does being grounded."

"Grounded?"

"It is a term used in the Craft. It means that you are connected to nature, and she to you. Most people who are not grounded suffer from physical symptoms such as vertigo, light-headedness, and a feeling of emptiness. They are out of touch with the earth's energy.

"Being out here also helps me to center myself. Centering is when you find inside of you a calm peacefulness. And that feeling stretches out around you before knitting itself into the pattern of the universe. Where you become one with everything around you." Morgan's eyes were closed as she said this, and I supposed that she was putting it into action, before she opened them to look at me.

"It is good to both ground and center yourself before and after each meditation. For, in meditation, you may often find yourself reaching a higher level than what you are used to. Grounding and centering afterward allows you to come back from that height and realize what has happened."

I nodded and asked her how to do these things. For the rest of the afternoon she taught me how to meditate. It was harder than I thought it would be.

After I learned to ground myself–imagining that there were roots of my own coming out of my feet and traveling deep into the earth–I was taught how to center. I did this by imagining that I was made of fine layers of thread and I was being woven into a blanket, making me one with everything else in the world.

Once this was accomplished, we had to focus on our breathing. Pull in a deep breath through the nose while counting to ten. Hold it for a count of ten. Let it exit through the mouth for a count of ten. And for all that time, that's all I should be concentrating on. But random thoughts would bounce back and forth through my head, making it hard to focus. I was told to acknowledge the thoughts as thoughts and to let them pass on by. And yet, I couldn't stop from adding more thoughts to the thoughts that were just there. It made it very difficult to empty my mind.

"Well, my dear, your fifteen minutes are up. It is best to meditate in the early morning. Before the excitements of the day keep your mind filled with thoughts and worries. Now, I want you to ground and center yourself once more."

I did as she asked, sending my bright, white roots into the center of the earth. I knitted myself into the universe, becoming one with all of the things around me. Becoming an invisible part of life.

Finally, I was done.

When I opened my eyes, it was still bright

out. This surprised me because it had felt much longer than fifteen minutes that I was meditating. And even adding the extra fifteen that grounding and centering had added on, it still felt like it should be almost dark. Looking at my watch, I realized that it was only three in the afternoon.

For a moment, we sat in the quiet of the garden and I looked around. When the sight was cut off, noises were more prominent. Now, with my eyes open, it was hard to hear all of the little things that I had been aware of only a moment before. Wind rustling through bushes was barely discernible now. A cat scratching itself in the windowsill was now unnoticeable. Things had dimmed down into a low hum of noise where nothing could be picked out and identified. I didn't like it.

"It is time for you to go, Alexandria."

I looked at Morgan to see her icy eyes unfocused. Was she seeing the future? Before I could ask, her eyes refocused on me and they had a sharpness to them. I nodded slowly and stood up. Out of the thousands of questions that I had, I knew they would have to wait.

"Thank you, Morgan. And you can call me Lex," I added with a smile. Then I turned and left the garden, stepping over the salt and closing the gate behind me.

As I rode my bike home, I suddenly wondered why I told her to call me Lex. Only my parents and myself used Lex. With everyone else I went by Alex. But Lex was special. Maybe I'd used it because what could be more special than her teaching me about magick? The thoughts stayed with me the entire way home.

Chapter Twenty

SWEET DREAMS

Morgan was right to send me home when she did. Just after I pulled my bike up to the shed, my dad's car pulled in the driveway. A grin split my face and I put my bike away before running to greet him at his car. When he got out, one arm reached out and caught me around the waist. I let out a shriek of laughter as he pulled me up and began to spin in place. And though his forearm was digging into my ribs, I didn't stop laughing until he set my unsteady feet back on the ground. Walking funny, we both staggered toward the house with our arms around one another.

"So, how'd you like the book? Have you studied it cover to cover yet?"

"Not yet. I only read one story so far," I answered as we walked through the front door. Mom came to the kitchen doorway and smiled at us.

"Oh really? What was it about?" he asked casually.

My mind began to race and I tried to come up with a piece of the truth that would keep Alyssa a secret. They didn't need to know about her. I didn't want them interfering with what she and I had. If they knew, maybe Alyssa would stop coming around.

"It's about a piano prodigy. Like Mozart. Only, they lived right here in Cedar Creek." I had to work to fill my voice with enthusiasm. My mom lifted an eyebrow as she came to greet us, a small smile on her face.

"Is that why you want to learn the piano so badly?"

"I asked to learn before Dad even gave me the book," I told her smartly and she laughed. "We signed me up for piano lessons today with Miss Catherine in town," I added to my father, this time genuinely excited.

"And when do you start?"

"Next Thursday at sixteen hundred."

My father smiled proudly at me and I knew that look was why it was dubbed 'Ryder Pride' by my mother. She certainly didn't have it the way Dad and I did. But I was right. Better to be proud of who you are than self-conscious of what you're not.

With the same look on my face, I turned with him and headed for the kitchen. It was a simple, normal evening for us after that. Dinner. Family time. Normalcy.

Later that night, however, I sat in the middle of my bed with my feet tucked under me. It wasn't the 'meditation pose' that I was sitting in, but close enough. My hands rested on my knees and I trailed my eyes around the room. Lowering my eyelids, I practiced my breathing and decided to try to meditate before bed.

This time, when I grounded myself, I imagined that the white cord was frayed at the ends. And those ends were tying themselves to everything in the earth. To flowers and the roots of trees. It burrowed under ponds and continued to the center of the earth. A feeling of being alive and strong filled me. That's what being grounded did. It made me feel like I was breathing in unison with everything else around me.

Now that I was grounded, I needed to work on centering myself. This image changed, too. Instead of thinking I was being knitted into the universe, I imagined it like a painting. And all of the paint was running together, pinks and blues melting into oranges and greens. All of it running over canvas. Just as every bit of energy ran into each other, melting and coming together.

That was what being part of the universe did. It gathered up all the colors and ran them together, mixing and clashing. Throwing together the least likely of combinations to make the most unique colors.

I was grounded, I was centered, and now I even had my breathing in sync. For about a whole minute and a half, I was successfully meditating. After five minutes of trying to block thoughts, however, I was getting sleepy. Before I knew it, my breathing acted as a sleeping agent and I was lying back.

I fell asleep.

This had to be a dream. For one, the room I was stand-

ing in was like mine, but with a dozen things moved around. There was no bathroom or closet. Instead, there was a large armoire and my desk, both in the corner where the sink and bathtub were in the waking world. Beside the armoire was my bed, directly across from the fireplace, which blazed cheerfully. This time with a crackle and pop as the wood burned.

Slowly, I turned to my right, toward the wall with the fireplace. In the corner between the west and north walls stood a rocking chair. The same creaky, old rocking chair that had been in my 'delusion' that one night. My mind was shaking from fear. Physically, however, I didn't react to it.

Turning to face the northern window, I noticed that there was the same kind of white gossamer curtain as what was in my room. Now, however, there were ivory/cream curtains embroidered with gold fleur-de-lis framing the windows. Underneath the window was an old-fashioned, rounded-top trunk. Like the kind in pirate stories. It was made out of cherry wood, giving it a distinct color. There was also a golden lock on it.

Making a full circle, I finally faced the wall behind me. I came face to face with Alyssa Rice!

She didn't react.

Without my permission, my eyes trailed down-

ward and looked at the vanity. Hands that were not mine reached down and picked up sheet music off of the vanity top. My eyes trailed unwillingly over the unfamiliar notes and black symbols covering line upon line. I yearned to look back in the mirror. To see Alyssa and know whether or not I was truly inside of her mind.

As if she heard me, Alyssa set down the sheets and picked up an old-fashioned hairbrush. The kind I had always liked but never had. Looking in the mirror, I watched as she—we—brushed the auburn ringlets that glowed copper in the firelight. For a whole minute and a half we did this and I was really starting to wonder why I was here.

Then it was gone.

I woke up the next morning, completely frustrated. Alyssa had gone beyond making contact last night. She'd actually pulled my subconscious into her memory. The worst of it was: I didn't even get to finish it.

At least I knew it wasn't from the night she died. She was wearing a blue dress and it had been bright daylight out. Still, just thinking of it clouded my head, making it ache just behind the ears.

Hoping to rid myself of the intrusive headache, I grounded and centered like I was supposed to—though I skipped my morning meditation. Yet, today was one of those days where I didn't want to deal with any of it. My dad was going to be home all day since it was Sunday, and I had every intention of leaving the mystery alone in favor of the blessed normalcy I'd had last night.

Chapter Twenty One

DEAL

Three days went by before I had any more contact with either Alyssa or Morgan. I had too much homework Monday and Tuesday night to be able to get out to the cottage in the woods. And Alyssa only made herself known when I was out on the swing in the backyard. She watched me from the attic, her chocolate eyes wide and pleading.

When Wednesday afternoon finally arrived, I was bouncing in my seat. I would be able to see Morgan. And once I saw her, I could finally tell her that I had been meditating at my desk every morning and was almost to the point where my mind could go completely blank for the whole fifteen minutes.

After saying hello to my mom and eating a quick snack, I was soon off. My bike plowed down the rain-softened road. Autumn was officially starting. The oak leaves were smattered with crimson, orange, and yellows. Some of them were already brown and falling from the trees. This created a crackly carpet all down the road. Mud stuck leaf after leaf to my tires and I knew that I would have to stop and pull them off before I got home. For now, I was too impatient to bother with them or the fiery tunnel I rode down. I wanted to see Morgan.

Parking my bike against the fence, I patted the gargoyles, opened the gate, stepped over the salt, and closed the gate again. This time, I looked to see if Morgan was waiting for me in the garden again. The bench was empty, its surface covered in the fresh rain. The Mother had taken the brunt of it, but the Maiden and Crone weren't entirely spared from the fresh water. Looking at the steel gray sky, I knew it was still threatening another wash later tonight.

For the third time, when I reached my hand up to knock, I was prevented from doing so. This time by the jade-eyed cat. She brushed my legs, her tail wrapping around it, before easing the thick door—which hadn't been latched properly—open. From inside, I heard Morgan's voice inviting me in. I sighed and gave up. I was simply not meant to rap my knuckles on the arched wooden door.

"Hello, Morgan," I said cheerfully as I came into the little house.

"Hello, Alexandria. You seem buoyant today," she observed with a small smile.

"I get to see you today," I answered. "And I thought today would be a good day for questions."

"Please, have a seat." There were two seats available. One was just a chest with a long cushion on it. The other was the rocking chair.

At first, I was going to pick the chest, hands down. Then I thought of me facing my fears and learning to play the piano. I had to get over my fear of rocking chairs, too. Yet, as I turned to sit in the aged wooden seat, I noticed the design on the top of the chair. It looked like simple scrollwork at first glance. But I recognized the climbing roses, made to crown whoever was sitting in the chair. Including nine year old girls. A cold chill swept through me and I immediately turned and sat on the bench, avoiding Alyssa's chair at all costs.

"What questions does your little heart hold for me? I'm sure you have many."

I sighed, trying to sort them all out in my head. "What is the salt line for?"

"Salt is believed to halt negativity. Those who wish you harm may not cross a salt line. The gargoyles, too, protect against evil. Which is why they are most common upon cathedrals and churches."

Well, there went my second question. Still, I had many more. "Why were you so surprised to find out that I was nine?"

Morgan smiled widely. "Nine, the completion of the greatest trinity in existence. Three is one of the most sacred numbers in the Craft. It is the number of the Goddess," Morgan said in a loving voice. She truly loved her Goddess. And, apparently, I was a prime numerical candidate for learning the Craft because I was full of trinities. (I think that's where this was going.)

"Can you tell me about the Goddess? Why is three her sacred number?" I asked quietly. My eagerness had given way to seriousness. She was right. Magick was no joke.

"Come with me," Morgan suggested and headed outside. I followed her the short distance to the bench. Somehow, I had a feeling I'd be looking at it again soon.

For a moment we stood in silence, the damp earth sending up an abundance of scents even as the wind pierced straight through my thin jacket. A few drops of water sprinkled from an overhanging branch and I caught them like tears on my cheeks. Still, nothing was said.

"Which one is the Goddess?" I finally asked.

"They all are." When she saw that I did not understand, Morgan continued. "They are the three phases of the Goddess. Each with their own phase of the moon. The Maiden serves as the waxing crescent–the one just growing into bloom. The Mother serves as the full moon–in the prime of existence. Giving life to the world in a different light. The waning crescent is for the Crone. The old woman whose time has passed and who has enjoyed life's numerous experiences." She said the last wistfully. As though she had missed something before reaching the crone stage of life.

"So, they are all three the Goddess at different stages in a woman's life?"

"Yes. She encompasses them all. Together and separate, she is all of them."

I waited expectantly and Morgan finally got the hint that I was eager for more. So she started to tell me things. After a lengthy lecture, which sort-of made my head spin, it was my turn to ask questions again. As we sat in the garden, I let my mind roam. It flew through my time in Cedar Creek and all of the strange things that had happened to me here. And I started to wonder how to use this witch thing to help with my Alyssa thing.

"What was your first power? What was the first thing you could do?" I asked shyly. I wasn't sure if she felt like answering so I only glanced up at her from time to time.

"The first thing that I could do? Hmm. I guess it would be my ability to predict the weather. From a very young age I was always able to tell what the weather would be like for weeks on end. As I got older, I actually learned to control it a bit. Yes. That was my first power."

I thought about this carefully. "What other kinds of powers are there?"

Before I got an answer, both of us looked toward the gate. It was like being with Morgan was already rubbing off on me. I could feel something getting closer. As I felt for them, I could suddenly feel the intense atmosphere around Morgan. The air seemed static next to her—as though the power inside of her was like lightning. The feeling coming closer to us was that of an iron bolt. Someone needed nerves like that if they were coming to this house. And somebody certainly was.

The feeling stopped right next to my bike. For one insane moment I was worried about vandalism. Then Morgan relaxed slightly, as though she knew the person, and my alarm vanished. Moving around Morgan slightly, I looked down the path to watch whoever it was come to the gate.

I was shocked by who appeared.

"Alex!" Nathan exclaimed as he stopped just on the other side of the gate.

"What are you doing here?" we demanded of each other in unison.

"Working," he said at the same time that I said, "Visiting." We both stared at each other like we were crazy. A second later, an uncomfortable silence fell over us. Before it was allowed to drag on, Morgan cleared her throat and our eyes shot to her face.

"I will return," she announced and walked into the house. As she left, I felt my feet edge toward the gate, so that I could better interrogate Nathan.

"What are you doing here, Alex?" he hissed as soon as the door of Morgan's cottage shut.

He kept darting glances over my shoulder. Surprisingly the iron bolt feeling emanating from him seemed to grow stronger rather than weaker from his fear.

"I'm just visiting. This isn't the first time I've talked to her. As you know," I added. Nathan glanced over my shoulder again. "Why are you here?"

"I'm delivering her mail," he said distractedly. My eyes widened.

"Why?" It was the first time I noticed that there was no mailbox on Old Grove Road.

"The mail carriers refuse to come down this far. Every Sunday I deliver her paper and every day after school I get her mail from the post office. And if she needs groceries, then she'll give me a list and money and I go and get those, too." His voice was a whisper.

I was stunned. "Why? Why do you do these things for her?"

"She doesn't go into town hardly at all. This is supposed to be my brother's job. But he passed it onto me as soon as he got it. He's too afraid to come near here."

"That's why you kept away when I first came here," I hissed, knowledge hitting me as I examined his motives. He'd been trying to stay out of sight of the cottage so that Morgan wouldn't know that he was part of my idiotic trespassing.

"Hello, Nathan. Here you are," Morgan said, suddenly appearing behind me. I jumped, as did Nathan. I saw a shiver run up his spine as he held out the two envelopes to Morgan and took one envelope in return. He eyed me meaningfully.

"Alexandria, perhaps it is time for you to go home. It will be raining inside of this very hour," Morgan told me with a serious voice, but her expression made me feel included. Because I knew what her first gift was. A smile split my face as I nodded my head.

"I will try to see you this weekend," I promised as I waved goodbye. Nathan sighed in relief as I walked out of the gate.

Retrieving our bikes, Nathan and I turned them quickly toward Norfolk Street. We each got on and began pedaling in silence. Silence was good. It helped me to think. However, the questions soon became too much for Nathan.

"What were you doing there, Alex? Seriously?"

I sighed. "I was visiting with her. She's really smart and I'm learning a lot from her."

"But she's a witch!"

"So?" I snapped back. "What does that have to do with anything?"

"What?" he gasped and looked over at me with wide green eyes.

"Listen, Nathan. I'm going to be spending a lot of my time with her. I like her. And I would appreciate it if no one else knew. I don't want to ruin what I have with her."

Nathan seemed to ponder that for a long time as we pedaled toward home. "Fine. I won't tell anyone. Just as long as you promise not to tell them about my job."

"Deal. We will never speak of this again."

"Deal," he repeated. We reached Norfolk Street and parted ways. Me to the left. Him to the right. And there's where we left most of our contact. Down Old Grove Road.

Chapter Twenty Two

HIDDEN KEY

I stepped inside the house just as it started to rain. Uncontrollably, I began to laugh. My mother heard me from the office and came into the kitchen. Crossing her arms, she leaned against the counter and studied me with a half-grin. Seeing that it was raining, she raised a single eyebrow at me.

"I just barely made it inside before it started to rain."

"Where are you spending all of your time lately, Lex?" she asked curiously. I'd have been really scared if I hadn't expected this question.

"I was at my friend Morgan's house," I answered honestly. My mother raised an eyebrow and I knew why.

"You never mentioned a Morgan. What about Becky, Amy, Mark, and Nathan?"

I shrugged. "Becky and Amy are petty. Mark follows them like a puppy. Nathan is okay. But Morgan is the best," I added cheerfully.

"Oh? And what makes her so special?"

I hesitated, as I knew there was a lot of explanation to be done. At the same time, I needed my mom to sign-off on me spending time with her *without* any mention of magick. This was going to be difficult...

"Well, for starters, she's an adult." Best to get that out there right away.

My mom's eyebrows shot into her hair and her eyes widened to the size of saucers. "She is?" It sounded like she wished for me to deny it.

"Yep. Remember that first day I pulled my bike out of the shed? When I went riding with the brat pack?" The nickname was new for me—and very disrespectful—but it fit the three acquaintances I wished to ditch.

Mom nodded, though I could see the slight glimmer of disapproval in her eyes. Pretending I didn't notice, I continued, "Well, we rode about half-way down Old Grove Road. There's only one house down the entire road and so I got curious. That's where I met Morgan." I was shortening the story, of course. No need to admit to all of my transgressions when Morgan obviously didn't mind them.

"And who, *exactly*, is Morgan?" my mother demanded, a hint of her mother-bear personality coming to light in her eyes.

"She's an older woman. I'd say she's in her sixties. Anyway, she has this really pretty garden and these cool stone gargoyles on her fence, and six cats. Morgan's nice, Mom. You'd like her," I urged. From the look in her eyes, however, I doubted I was having much luck.

"Alexandria, you know you're not supposed to talk to strangers. And you are most definitely not supposed to be in their yards. This is not how I expect you to behave when you leave this house," she scolded.

My head hung and I couldn't meet her eyes. At the same time, I was really glad that she didn't know the full story. Of course, there was still one way for me to get out of this almost in a full piece.

"I'm sorry, Mom. I know that I'm not supposed to approach strangers, but I felt sorry for her. Morgan's a hermit. She doesn't leave her own house and has everything delivered to her. The kids around here... Well, they're cruel. They make fun of her and call her things that they have no business talking of. Yes, I behaved wrong in how I made friends with her. But I don't think making friends with her was a wrong decision at all."

Turning on my heel, I strode out of the kitchen and made my way hurriedly to my room. I wasn't often one for dramatic exits, but if they helped my cause, I knew how to use them to my advantage. Knowing my mother as I did, she would stew for some time over my behavior, but eventually she would feel guilty for scolding me—at the same time unconsciously acknowledging that it would really do no good, anyway. After all, the damage was done. The only thing she could really do was embrace it.

With that knowledge in mind, I entered into my bedroom and was about to make my way to the desk when I paused. From the corner of my eye, I caught such a quick flash of orange light that it was gone before I knew for sure it existed.

Whipping my head to the left, all I could think was, *Of course!*

Dropping to my hands and knees, I was all eagerness as I peered into the fireplace. No fear enveloped me as I reached a hand inside and began to feel at the white-painted bricks. Methodically, I traced each mortared avenue between the stones, looking for a false sealant or loose brick. None fell into my hands however and I let out a disappointed exhale. Retrieving my hand from the uppermost corners, I jerked it out hurriedly when something strange brushed my wrist.

As I rubbed the spot where something small and kind-of slimy had brushed my skin, I leaned my head further into the fireplace. Moving with caution, I inched my fingers up the inside of the face of the fireplace. Since it was one solid piece of stone, there were no bricks for me to pry at here. But there was a gap where there shouldn't have been.

Again, that same feeling attacked my fingers, but I grasped at it this time. A smile flitted onto my face as I realized it was an old bit of leather. Pulling gently, I was able to free the object it was tied to and brought it out into the light. Resting in my open palm was a large, brass key.

For several moments, I stared at it in delight, unable to believe my good fortune. I'd found it! The key to the attic and the way into Alyssa's hiding place. Once the surprise wore off, I leapt to my feet, ready to run off and find her that very instant.

Then my face paled as I heard my mom's distinctive footsteps reach the top of the stairs and turn toward my room. Dropping to all fours, I thrust my hand back up into the unused fireplace and returned the key to its hiding space. And just as she reached the outside of my bedroom door, I sprinted into my bathroom and began to wash the dirt and cobwebs from my hands.

Blessedly, when my mom came in to talk to me, it was not a long conversation. She repeated again why what I did went against what both my parents had constantly expressed as good behavior. The dangers of doing such things, and so on. In the end, however, she conceded that she could find no reason why I could not continue my friendship with Morgan—under the condition that both of my parents meet her. Since it was not my place to argue it, I had to agree. Morgan would surely understand the necessity of it.

Once these points were made, my mother then asked me to come downstairs and help her with dinner. My heart sank in my chest and I almost shot a glance to the fireplace. The urge to solve this mystery was running through my veins at top speed and I wanted nothing more than to grab the key and run straight to the attic door. But I couldn't. Because my mother was entitled to spend time with me. So, with as large a smile as I could manage, I gave up my obsession in favor of my responsibilities.

Later that night, I lay in my bed staring at the fireplace. The itch to just jump out of bed and get it all over with was practically causing me to twitch. But my parents weren't in bed yet, and I was pretty sure any scurrying noises going on up here would send one or the other up to me. Not a good idea.

When I was finally able to give up the idea as a lost cause, I rolled onto my right side and focused on the northern wall. It took all of my willpower not to roll back over. For several minutes, I stared at the wall with no sight of anything. Until I realized that, in Alyssa's time, I would have been looking in her mirror.

Thinking her name was all it took.

We were back in her room again, but close to the door this time. Her pale white hand reached out and picked up the sheet music off of the desk. With her other hand, Alyssa grabbed a large, brass key. Opening the door, I was carried off in Alyssa's mind as we headed for the door that had failed me.

Passing a mirror in the hall, I couldn't help but stop and look. Somehow, I wasn't sure that it was my curiosity that stopped us. Rather, I think it was Alyssa's vanity. She primped her auburn curls and smoothed her green dress. Suddenly, she threw back her shoulders, lifted her chin, turned and off we went.

The brass key she was holding slipped immediately into the lock and turned delicately. Once inside the room, Alyssa grabbed a snow globe off of the shelves that were embedded in the wall to the left of the stairwell. After twisting the little knob underneath, a lullaby began to filter through the air. It only lasted if the thing was held. Alyssa, not caring about the melody or the pretty snow globe, set it in the middle of the stairs.

Being in her head, I knew that this was her alarm system. Should a servant or her parents enter, they would pick it up and place it aside. The music would go off and give Alyssa proper warning of their approach.

Smiling in satisfaction, Alyssa stepped around the snow globe and began to tread softly up the attic steps, carrying me in her mind. She looked up and I could see the light from the windows fill up the blackness.

And that was it.

I woke up.

Chapter Twenty Three

PIANO LESSON

I couldn't have been more frustrated when I woke up. This was worse than finding that I couldn't get into the attic *and* that first cut-off dream I had with Alyssa. What was even more provoking was that I never seemed to get enough sleep when I was dreaming with her. It was like I was still awake, just somewhere in the past.

As it was, I still had school and my piano lesson to deal with. I didn't have time to ponder what dreaming with Alyssa meant. Although, I did have to admit that I was glad we'd picked up contact again. Whether because of Morgan or because of my attempt at learning what she loved, I didn't know.

"Baby, what's wrong?" my mother asked. Too

late, I realized I was scowling.

"Nothing. I just can't wait for this school day to be over with," I muttered.

"Are you really that excited about piano lessons?" she asked with true curiosity. For the first time I had to wonder how this looked to my mother. A nine-year-old girl, who had a history of being outdoors during all daylight hours, now willingly shutting herself up to practice the piano.

Alright, that was a stretch.

"Yes. I actually can't wait," I admitted with a smile. My mother's lips curled in the corners before she pressed them to my forehead.

"You better hurry, the bus will be here soon." I nodded and quickly emptied my cereal bowl before trotting out to the end of the gate. I was just in time.

Nathan sat with me on the bus again. It was normal now. No one wanted to sit with the girl who ignored their questions about the witch. I was perfectly fine with that and was content to stare out the window all through the bus ride. Yet, there was just a little something different today.

For the first time, I paid attention to the people who got on the bus with Nathan. One was a girl of about six years named Jenny. Another was her twin, Jessie. The third person to get on the bus with Nathan was taller than he was. At least two years older than us, and much more arrogant. This was Tyler. Nathan's older, cowardly brother. I smiled to myself a bit and turned to look out the window. Only Tyler, Nathan, Morgan, and I knew that Tyler was too chicken to go near Morgan's house. And Nathan was brave enough to stand it. For the first time since coming here, I was certain that I had at least two acquaintances to be proud of.

The rest of the day passed more irritatingly. School was boring. I got loaded with homework. And Becky was being a stuck-up brat during our class assignment. Amy rubbed off on her *way* too much. Still, two things were constantly bugging me all day: the key and the piano lesson. One had to come before the other, obviously. But this weekend was going to be something entirely different.

Almost as soon as the doors opened, I was running down the bus steps and through the gate. Trotting over the stepping stones, I almost fell a couple of times but kept going. I was in a hurry and nothing would slow me down.

"Hey Mom," I said cheerily as I came into the kitchen. Maybe, if I was lucky, I would have just enough time to snag the key before my piano lesson.

"Hey, baby. You seem to be doing better," she commented with a wide smile.

"School's over," I said with a shrug and sat down at the table where crackers with peanut butter between them awaited me. My mother laughed as she sat down beside me.

"Excited for this afternoon?"

"Definitely. I hope it's not too hard," I added with a frown. I was thinking about retrieving the key. She thought I was talking about the piano.

"Kids all over the world think that it is a boring waste of time. And you just hope that it's not too hard to learn? How did I end up with the strangest kid in America?"

"You're just lucky, I guess."

"Well, my lucky Lex, I'm going to be in the office and update the computers a bit, since we've got an hour before your lesson. Try not to run off," she added with a smile.

"Morgan can go without me for a day, I think," I responded with a bigger grin. She kissed my head and walked out of the room.

I didn't waste a second.

Abandoning my afterschool snack, I slunk through the house until I reached the second story. Retrieving the key from its hiding place in my room, I almost ran to the attic door. With my teeth pressed deep into my bottom lip, I slipped the brass object into the keyhole and turned it slowly. The resounding click caused me to exhale through my mouth and a huge grin grew on my face.

Again, the footsteps interrupted my moment of triumph. With a glare full of venom, I locked the door again and thrust the key behind my back just as my mom reached the top of the stairs.

"There you are," she said. "Your piano teacher called. There was a permanent cancellation, so your lessons have been moved up half an hour. Why don't you go grab your coat and we'll head out."

I nodded with as much of a smile as I could manage as I headed back to my bedroom. As soon as the door closed behind me, I let out a frustrated exhale. This was going to be a long day. At least, however, I was finally going to get over that ridiculous fear that Alyssa had given me.

"Alright. That was a great first lesson," Miss Catherine complimented me.

"Thanks," I yawned. Miss Catherine chuckled and stood up from the bench.

"Now, at least try to learn these until our next lesson. I know it has to be difficult, what with school and everything, but it's very rewarding for those who are dedicated to learning," she said in a kindly voice. I nodded, smiling.

At the same time, I was groaning in my head. Great. Homework. Piano work. And I still had to figure out everything with Alyssa and spend time with Morgan.

My mom walked over as soon as we were done and asked if I was ready to go home. I nodded and ended up yawning again. She smiled and led me out to the car. I waved goodbye to my teacher before leaving.

Of course, I could not be more surprised

than when my mother passed our road. Perking up in an instant, my eyes widened as we turned down Old Grove Road. Despite the surprise it would cause, I smiled. My mom was going to meet Morgan. It was her irrevocable way of saying that she approved my friendship with her and would no longer interfere—so long as she knew I was safe.

Chapter Twenty Four

THE ATTIC

My chance to enter the attic didn't come until Saturday morning.

I didn't dream like I expected. No more flashes. Alyssa was forcing me to find out on my own what was in that attic. Of course, that undoubtedly meant that I was waking up as the false dawn pretended to light up my windows.

Crawling out of bed, I padded quietly to my north window. Outside, the world went from black to blue and the mourning doves were beginning their eerie calls. Opening the window, I let the breeze carry in the sweet smell of the flowers in the garden. The scent of the ivy overpowered it all as I leaned out of the window just a bit. The breeze rustled the leaves, adding to the song of the doves and I closed my eyes to enjoy the moment. It came to an end too quickly.

Chills began to prickle the skin of my arms and I pulled the window closed. Turning, I began to make my bed, knowing that I wasn't going to be sleeping anymore. As I was fitting the sheets, I lifted my pillow and noticed the key.

Biting my lip, I began to debate. Glancing at my window, I watched as false dawn was slowly leaching away, a true dawn taking its place. My dad would wake up the second the first rays of light entered their bedroom. Mom would follow not long after. Yet, neither expected me to be up so early.

Making a decision, I dressed quickly and snatched the key from my bed. Easing out into the hallway, I looked both ways as if I was crossing a street. Seeing and hearing nothing, I slipped from my room and made my way to the mysterious attic door. It was now or never.

Déjà vu swept over me as the key entered the lock and turned delicately. The door swung open, revealing the staircase with the shelves. There, sitting innocently upon the stair was the snow globe. Inside was a red brick house coated in green ivy. Taking a slow step toward it, I lifted it off the stair.

Instantly, music began to play and I hurriedly twisted the key on the bottom and set the globe back on the stairs. The music stopped and I stood listening to every noise in the house to be sure I hadn't woken my parents. After a few minutes, I breathed a sigh of relief and took the key from the door. Turning on the light, I closed the door behind me.

Staring up the stairs, I felt like I was back in Alyssa's head. Except for the fact that Alyssa had been up here during daylight, so that the attic was lit up by sunshine. Instead, I had the lousy yellow lights to guide my way. My lips puckered as I stared at the bulbs that looked like they could burn out at any second. *Oh well. Now or never.*

Slowly, I began to walk up the wooden steps, careful to avoid excessive creaking. The light coming through the window was added to the yellow light bulb as I inched upwards. I kept my eyes on my feet as I neared the top. I didn't want to know, yet, what was waiting for me. Also, I had a fear of looking up, seeing Alyssa, and falling down. Who could blame me?

Finally, I reached the top of the stairs. Gulping, I slowly raised my eyes from the floor to the window. Alyssa wasn't there, which made me feel a little better.

Gaining more bravery, I allowed my eyes to trail away from the window to the left. There, covered with a white sheet, sat Alyssa's vanity. The dust on the floor around it made it appear that it hadn't been moved in a long, long time. Nothing in the attic had been moved in a long time.

My eyes moved once more, taking in the rest of the attic space. Everything was covered with white sheets, making some objects indistinguishable. It looked like an easel was over in the corner, and a table was against the wall. And to the right of the room, there appeared to be a large, strange-looking object.

A suspicion entered my mind and I inched over to it. Reaching a hand out tentatively, I gripped the sheet and tugged on it gently. It slid off of the object, fluttering smoothly to the floor. There before me stood Alyssa's harp.

It was big for an adult, much less a nine-year-old. Gilded in gold, roses climbed all over the instrument. Beautiful and intimidating, I almost didn't touch it. Almost.

Afraid of making a loud enough noise to alert my parents, I stretched out and plucked one of the thin strings, sending out a haunting note into the atmosphere. Immediately, I stepped back.

Turning, I went to pull the sheet off of the other objects in the room. I'd have to clean up here later. Maybe when my dad went to work one day. My mom had papers to grade, so I could get away with it. Maybe.

Tables, a couple of straight-back chairs, an easel and the padded seat for the vanity. After pulling the sheets off of all of these, I gulped and pulled the sheet off of the vanity. As I did so, I knocked something to the floor. After pulling the white fabric to the side, I bent down to pick up the fallen object. It turned out to be an ornate hair piece.

An intricate golden roses hairband. Perfect for pushing back curls off of a performer's face. My breathing stopped as I slowly stood up. So, this is where she'd come when she left the party. But where did she go from here?

As I turned to the vanity to place the hairpiece back, I glanced into the mirror. Automatically, I gasped and stumbled backwards. Alyssa lifted a finger to her lips. My blood ran cold, goosebumps rising all over my body and the hairs on the back of my neck standing straight up. The finger fell from her mouth and the girl giggled before disappearing entirely.

"Not funny," I managed to mutter at the seemingly empty room. My body was still reacting, so I knew that she was still there.

Turning back to the vanity, I studied the objects laid on it. The hairpiece. A brush and comb. Even a little container of what I thought was makeup. My nose scrunched up at that, thinking of my cousin who was always in beauty pageants. Then I found something quite strange.

A silver picture frame. Picking it up, I had enough light in the room to examine the two girls. One was sitting in a rocking chair, crowned with carved roses. She was dressed luxuriously with perfect ringlets hanging around her face. Alyssa. The other was standing to her right, staring into the camera with a gleam in her dark eyes. Black hair hung down her back and she was wearing a dark dress that hung to her knees. There was something just so familiar about her...

Yet, that was nothing in the face of what I realized only a second later. My eyes flashed around the room, searching for the missing object. It wasn't there. Of course not. Because Morgan had it. The rocking chair really was one in the same.

Anger filled me as I set the picture down and ended up running down the stairs. Picking up the snow globe, I thrust it back on its shelf, yanked the door open, turned off the light, and ran out. After shutting the door and locking it, I ran to my room to get my shoes and coat. It was time to confront my teacher.

Chapter Twenty Five

CONFRONTATION

"Lex? Where are you going this early?" my mother asked in a perplexed tone.

"Morgan's," was all I said and ran out the kitchen door. I barely paused to pull my bike out of the shed. I could've run the distance I was so angry. But the bike was faster.

As I came to a stop outside of Morgan's house, I flung my bike off of the road. If I hadn't been boiling, I'd have felt chagrinned. I was taught to always take care of my belongings. Storming toward the gate, I thought about barging up to her door and pounding on it until she answered.

I didn't make it very far.

As I reached out a hand to push open the gate, I was frozen. My hand would stretch no further, and my feet were rooted to the ground. It was as if I had run straight into an invisible wall.

Standing there, my heart was beating wildly and I glanced about in a panic. Looking to my left and right, I soon realized that something had changed. There was something different about the gate itself. Then I realized what it was...

The gargoyles were staring at me! Literally staring at me. Their bulldog heads were turned in my direction and their expressions could only be described as stern. I wasn't getting through. Not in the mood I was in. Even the salt line was glowing with a luminescent light. Until I calmed down, no negativity was going to be able to cross into Morgan's world.

Sighing, I did something I never thought I would do. First, I turned and picked up my bike and leaned it gently against the fence that surrounded her property. Then, I went and sat cross-legged in front of the gate and began to ground, center, and meditate.

For maybe an hour I was out there. It was hard, at first, to get over my anger. The need for answers was just as potent as the questions that needed answering. After a while, however, the curiosity beat out the anger and frustration. Everything else disappeared in the face of that rampant desire for answers. That set me free.

After grounding and centering once more, I stood up slowly and took a step toward the gate. The gargoyles had returned to their previous positions while my eyes were closed and the salt stopped glowing. Just as I was about to push open the gate, Morgan appeared from nowhere and opened it for me. I admit, I jumped.

"H-hello," I stammered. She tilted her head to the side. "How did you know I was here?"

"Towel fell." That was all she said. I nodded, knowing that she was serious.

Morgan then stepped aside and I slowly stepped over the salt line and through the gate. Silently, I followed her through the dawn light to her cottage. I watched the lavender smoke rise gently and curl toward the heavens. Inside, I wished I could do that. Float to the sky and worry about nothing. How peaceful would that be?

"You are not here on a friendly visit, I conclude. What reason did you have for setting off the gargoyles?" she asked as she opened the door.

I followed her inside timidly. Would I get kicked out if I got angry again?

"The same reason I ran from my house before the sun is all the way up. Why do you have her chair?" I said in as strong of a voice as I could manage. With Morgan's cold blue eyes on me, it was kind-of difficult.

"Ah. So it is with anger and confusion that you come to my house in an hour in which we should both be meditating and preparing to meet the new day with open-mindedness and acceptance." There was a hint of a smile on her face.

"Yes. I want to know what you know. I *need* to know what you know."

"And why is that, young Alexandria?" she asked, turning and sitting in the chair she had sat in before. I stood, standing beside the rocking chair. I was still afraid to touch it. Especially now that I knew it was the very same one.

For a moment, I debated how to answer. Morgan wouldn't allow me to lie to her. I wouldn't allow me to lie to her. So, I had to tell her the truth. I had to tell her my secret. It was time to tell her about Alyssa.

"I need to know what happened to Alyssa

Rice. I need to know why her rocking chair is in your house. You know something. I know you do."

"Alyssa Rice, you say?" she asked, her words whipping out like steel cables, entrapping me. I nodded silently. "What do you know about her?"

"She's dead, for one thing," I responded, not liking the way she was making me feel. Morgan's icy eyes bored into me as she stood up. Her tall frame hovered over mine.

"What else?" There was no way to get around her demand.

Hanging my head, I relented. I told her everything about Alyssa. In the end, I felt like I'd betrayed her. She shared herself with me. Not anyone else. And here I had told Morgan everything. It left me feeling hollow.

"Stay away from that attic, Alexandria," Morgan said in a calm voice when I had finished speaking. I felt my jaw set stubbornly.

"No," I growled. "She needs me. I'm not going to abandon her."

"You will do as I say."

"No!" I yelled. "I don't care if you never teach me to use magick. Alyssa came to me. She needs me. Never leave a man behind. That's what I was taught. I'm not leaving her."

"Alyssa will hurt you," Morgan snapped in a clear voice that cut over all of my hysterics. My mouth snapped shut. The instinct for self-preservation was much higher than even my stubbornness would have imagined.

"How do you know?" I demanded, my chin jutting out in a pigheaded gesture.

"Some spirits don't care what they do to the human body, Alexandria. Alyssa certainly does not since she's deemed it fit to enter your mind. Show you things you are too inexperienced to see, to know. She will hurt you if you continue to make contact with her." Morgan was deathly serious but I was too stubborn.

"Obviously someone has already hurt her because she was left alone. Someone needs to find out what happened to her. It may as well be me."

"No, Alexandria. You've not learned enough in order to stave off the effects making contact with her will have on you. We take care of the living first. The dead must wait their turn. Have patience. Learn well. And you both shall have your just reward. Knowledge."

Tears were filling my eyes and I shook my head. But it was in defeat. If Alyssa could hurt me, then I had to protect myself. Obviously she didn't realize that the things she showed me could harm me. She wouldn't intentionally hurt me. Would she?

Chapter Twenty Six

PSYCHOMETRY

I wasn't sure what I was expecting. For Morgan to tell me that I should just leave? For Alyssa to show up and promise that she wouldn't show me anything harmful anymore? I wasn't sure. All I knew was that the room was spinning and my legs were shaking. I reached out a hand to steady myself.

It wasn't the best idea.

Faintly, I recognized the smooth texture of aged wood beneath my palm. As my fingers curled around it, I realized what it was: the top of the rocking chair. But I was too hazy to deal with the shock.

White mist clouded over my eyes and I couldn't see. My pulse began to pound in my head, drowning out everything else. Suddenly, the mists retreated to the edges of my vision. A woman who looked to be about twenty-three sat in the rocking chair with a bundled infant in the crook of her left arm. Her black hair was in a thick braid, with wisps escaping it around her face. It appeared that I was looming down on her and her head whipped toward me and her eyes locked onto mine. She looked surprised and frightened. Just as suddenly, the white mist closed over the image before I regained my sight. With a gasp, I yanked my hand away from the rocking chair, glaring at the polished wood.

"What was that?" Morgan and I exclaimed at the same time.

"I don't know," I yelled back, frightened. Morgan ushered me to the chest I had sat on before.

"What did you see, Alexandria?" Morgan demanded in a stern tone

In broken words, I tried to explain. "I saw the girl from the picture. The one with the raven hair. Only, she was all grown up with a baby in her arms. She looked up and she was frightened."

"Alexandria, I think you should ask your

parents if you can spend the night here." My eyes widened at her implication.

"I don't know if they'll let me. My mom just met you and my dad hasn't met you yet. They're pretty strict about where I spend the night."

"Regardless, I need you here tonight. I've been remiss in your training. We need to start immediately."

I felt my brows pull together suspiciously. "What are you talking about? You know what just happened to me, don't you?" I demanded.

"It is a fairly rare gift called psychometry. It is the ability to obtain knowledge about an event or person by touching objects related to either. You see the history of objects. It is uncommon and often misjudged. People have little patience for history anymore. Therefore, most never go on to expand their ability. I've never seen someone with such a strong gift as yours, Alexandria."

After absorbing all of that for a minute, I only had one question, "Do you have a phone?"

"I keep one for emergency purposes, though it is often unplugged," Morgan said with a small smile as she dug out an old, heavy, roll-dial phone. I grinned at the ancient thing and wondered if it still worked.

"Okay then."

Sighing, I picked up the phone and heard the obnoxious dial tone. Slowly, making sure I got the numbers right, I placed my finger into the first hole and rolled it around. When it stopped, I removed my finger and moved on to the next one. After a while, the numbers were all in and the phone dialed my house number.

"Ryder residence," my mother said as she answered the phone. I almost gulped.

"Hey Mom," I said shyly.

"Lex!" she exclaimed. "Where are you? Why did you leave so early? Are you okay? What's going on?" I pulled away from the receiver a little at her demanding tone.

"Relax, Mom. I'm fine. I just wanted to see Morgan. Sorry if I scared you," I said repentantly. I heard my mother sigh in relief that I was alright and everything.

"The next time you decide you want to go to Morgan's—or anywhere else—you need to ask permission. I can't be wondering if someone died the next time you run out of the house."

"Okay. I'm really sorry," I said, leaving a

pause at the end.

"What do you want, Alexandria?" my mother asked in a no-nonsense tone.

"Um... Speaking of permission... Can I spend the night here?" I asked in a cautious tone, expecting a rebuff.

"Lex," my mother sighed dramatically.

"I'm sorry. Really," I added quickly. "But please, Mom?"

"Is there something going on that I should know about, Alexandria?" she asked in a warning tone.

"Of course not, Mom. I'm just going to be here all day and don't want to be riding my bike home after sunset," I said, playing on my safety. My mother sighed again, but she sounded defeated this time. I forced the grin from my face.

"No, I don't want you riding at night, either. Fine. Just as long as it is alright with Morgan, you can spend the night."

"Thanks Mom! She already said it was okay. I love you. See you bright and early tomorrow morning," I exclaimed and hung up before she could say anything other than a quick, "I love you, too."

"That was brief," Morgan replied as I placed the receiver in the cradle.

"It's best not to give my mom wiggle-room when it comes to a decision. She can wiggle out of any choice. Dad and I are too stubborn to wiggle out. We see stuff through to the end. Although, that includes a lot of bad decisions. Mom knows how to wiggle out of those. But Dad and I ... don't."

Morgan chuckled. "You see so brightly for a child of such few years," she replied, placing a long, thin finger under my chin and lifting my head higher so that I could meet her gaze.

"Even the past," I added, staring into her icy irises.

"That you do, Lex. That you do," she murmured.

"So what can you teach me?"

"Let us begin."

Chapter Twenty Seven

INFLUENCE

Though nearly impossible, I did as Morgan asked. Each and every day, I pulled myself from Alyssa's influence. It was torturous some days. She was so strong.

But it was for the best.

After only a week, I was already so much more clear-headed. Meditation and psychic shields took up most of that time. In my own home, they were all I could indulge in. It changed me. Matured me. Magick ... it flowed through me. In the end, it made me a stronger, more aware individual.

But I barely got to touch it.

Before I could learn magick, I first had to learn the rules of magick. I'd never done more speed-reading in one week than what I had accomplished at Morgan's house. Herbs, astrology, magick, stones, runes, tarot, and animals. All filled my head like a giant swirl. It was well worth it.

Especially when I came across a book describing the different types of ESP—extrasensory perception. Psychometry was in the book. Along with a close relative of it: retrocognition, meaning the ability to view past events without the aid of an object. Pyrokinesis, hydrokinesis, aerokinesis, and geokinesis were all the abilities to control elements. Fire, water, air, and earth.

Also, there was psychokinesis; which was the ability to affect matter with only the mind. Telekinesis fell under this category. It was a gift I was most anxious to learn. Yet, I was barred from starting on it just yet.

"All things in time," Morgan would say. Along with, "Patience is the most rewarding of all gifts. This you must learn first, Alexandria."

Perhaps the one ability I was most anxious to learn, however, was how to create a glamour. It was best described as a lie for the eyes. An illusion. In one year, it was my mission to be able to learn this fascinating ability.

The week passed and I found myself sitting at the piano Friday afternoon. It was always hardest to block Alyssa while I was sitting at the piano. And yet, I felt so much more mature sitting there. Rather like I was thirteen instead of nine.

"Practicing?" my Mom asked as she came into the room. Suddenly I was nine years old again as I turned to grin at her.

"Yes. I'm not improving much," I admitted as I turned back to the open book with the notes for A, B, C, D, and E on it. Scrunching up my nose, I attempted to hit them while trying to make it sound more like music and less like noise.

"Good luck. Not all things are learned at once. Have patience," she said with a smile, kissing the top of my head before walking toward the office.

Sighing, I continued to practice. Suddenly, I hit a cold spot with my left hand. I sucked the air through my teeth as I fought off the white mist that threatened my vision. Already, I knew that it would show me Alyssa playing the notes flawlessly. But that's not what I needed. This was something I had to learn on my own. Throwing a psychic shield up around me, I proceeded to practice.

The cold spot didn't go away. In fact, it began to move with my left hand. Once, the key was pressed without me even applying pressure to it. I glared at it, knowing that I couldn't see Alyssa in order to glare properly at her.

Stop it, I hissed mentally at her. At the same time, I pushed out my psychic shield to cover all of me. The cold spot receded. Almost instantly, I felt the angry sting of rejection coming from beside me. It was something so strong and unexpected, I dropped the psychic shield instantly.

She was in my head faster than I could blink. The white mist shrouded my vision until it retreated to the edges. The image I saw was one that I was extremely uncomfortable with.

At first, my eyes were closed. But I could feel my fingers moving. They were playing out a haunting, rich, exquisite melody. It was utterly magickal. As I opened my eyes, I was amazed by how fast my tiny fingers flew over the ivory keys. My ringlets fell across my shoulders as I was absorbed into the music. Life wound up in those transcending notes and got caught in the cordial pitches. I was sharing my heart and soul with those around me, all in the very sound of music.

Then the song ended on a haunting note and I looked up. It was the day Alyssa died. The ivory dress flowed down to my knees as I stood up and bowed. I smiled in faux-appreciation. But I couldn't feel anything other than the desire to have them all gone. To just disappear and not come back.

The white mist covered my eyes once more as the vision suddenly disappeared. I shook my head, feeling relief come from beside me. I glowered at the empty space to my left. The shield I threw up now was stronger than ever before. It was almost visible, that thick wall that separated me from her. Angry rejection stabbed at me again before Alyssa's presence faded. Automatically, I knew she'd gone to sulk in the attic.

Feeling frustrated myself, I turned back to the piano. I had to finish my practice before I was allowed to leave for Morgan's. I was spending the night with her and needed to get my things together. She would scold me for my lack of control, I was sure. But I knew she would be interested to learn that I was beginning to form the ability to become an empath. I could now feel what others were feeling. Well ... I could feel what Alyssa was feeling.

As practice ended, I had to wonder if I could now register my mother's feelings. Did this new ability work only on Alyssa? Or the living as well as the dead?

Casually, I wandered to the office my mother was tucked away in. She was grading papers again, I noticed. Before I even made it into the room, I could feel her frustration mixed with her never-ending patience. That red pen was getting too much use on that one paper, apparently.

"Mom? I'm done practicing. I'm going to gather my things and head to Morgan's before the sun sinks any lower. Thanks for letting me go," I said in a quiet, hurried voice. I left before she had time to do more than lift her head and look at me.

My overnight backpack was packed and kept under the stairs. I grabbed it and hurried out to the shed. I wanted to leave before my dad got home and could detain me. Morgan needed to know what was going on. She was the only one I could tell. At this point, she was the only one I could trust.

Chapter Twenty Eight

EFFECT

"You're here earlier than I expected," Morgan said as I strode through the gate. I tried to smile at her. She raised an eyebrow at me and I sighed in defeat.

Straightening up, she peeled off her gardening gloves and set them next to the small shovel she'd been using. Wiping her forehead with the back of her hand, she motioned me to the bench. As always, she sat on the Crone's side. I sat on the Maiden's. Both of us carefully avoided the ivy tendril I had noticed my first time in Morgan's garden. Lacing her fingers together over her knee, Morgan looked at me expectantly.

"I failed," I stated in a strong, calm voice. "I let the shield drop and she got to me."

Morgan sighed and shook her head at my defeat. I felt like a loser and stared at the ground.

"What happened?" she questioned. I immediately launched into the description of events, as I knew them. For a long time, she remained silent.

I stared at her in the silence. It was more than just trying to read her perfectly blank expression, though. My body was picking up all of the emotions running through her. When I'd first started talking, disappointment had been plain. That had faded into curiosity which held steady throughout the story. Now, however, I felt nothing but concern emanating from the woman beside me.

"Why do my new powers concern you?" I asked in a casual tone.

"I am your teacher. Whatever happens to you concerns me," she answered. Though she was correct, I felt like she knew what I was really talking about and had just dodged my question.

"I didn't mean that. I can feel you. You're not frustrated or curious anymore. And it's not full-out worry. It's just ... concern."

"Yes. I am concerned over your developing

powers. And do you know why?"

I shook my head no. Morgan's icy eyes bored into mine.

"All of your gifts seem to be appearing after contact with Alyssa. It is something that troubles me. Your first experience as a Medium was at night shortly after you moved in. Your first retrocognitive experience was when Alyssa took you back in time through her memories. Which, in turn, set off your psychometry, I believe. Now, after sitting in one of her most active locations, you are now empathic. It is something to be concerned over, that she is the trigger for your gifts to manifest."

I thought about that for a long time. Both of us drifted back into silence as we pondered Alyssa's role in my life. After a while, Morgan shifted and looked into my eyes, hers piercing into my soul.

"We must redouble your training. The sooner you learn to control your powers, the sooner we can be done with Alyssa Rice."

"Why do you hate her so much, Morgan?" I asked quietly. "As far as I can see, the most she's done is try to show me what happened to her. Is that so bad?"

"It is when you are but a child, Alexandria. As I've said before: her antics can harm you. I'd rather not have you in harm's way. Alyssa may or may not know what she does to you, but I would not risk you just to find her truth."

"I would," I muttered, knowing it would do no good. Morgan lifted a brow and I looked away. "What do you wish to teach me today?"

"Since I am working in the garden, why do we not review your terminology?" she asked with a small smile. I tried to smile back, but terminology over a new power wasn't something that would really excite me. Still, I followed her back to the plants.

"This one?" she asked, pointing out a small clump of white flowers that had six petals each. I smiled with confidence.

"An eagle or wild garlic," I announced. Morgan smiled slightly and raised an eyebrow in a sly fashion.

"Do you also know the Latin term?" I raised both eyebrows and shook my head. "There is a book in my house that you should read. How about this one?"

"Bloody fingers or foxglove," I answered.

"This one?"

"Archangel or angelica."

"And this one?"

"Absinthe or wormwood."

The quiz went on and on. The first words out of my mouth were the old terms. From the days when witches were burned at the stake or tied to stones and drowned in lakes. They were the everyday terms back then. Those second words I spoke were the everyday words for this time.

And though I'd rather be learning about my gifts, I did have fun expanding my knowledge of the plants and the old language. It made me feel like a real witch from the old days. I could imagine myself dressed in long skirts and old cloaks just like Morgan. To feel like a real witch is what I wanted.

After an hour of practicing, and getting most of the answers correct, the sun was setting. Gathering up the tools, we stored them in a wooden box outside of her house that held spare chopped wood along with other gardening supplies. Seeing the wood there, it began to make me wonder about Morgan's powers. Again.

Instead of questioning her fruitlessly, I followed her inside and washed up, placing my bag in a corner. Then we sat down in our places while she lit some candles. All of the ones she lit were purple, to induce peace and tranquility. Also, purple was the color of spiritual enlightenment. I waited patiently as I pulled out my sleeping bag.

"Morgan?" I asked tentatively.

She turned to me with a peaceful expression. "Yes?"

I took a deep breath, preparing for the insolent question I was about to ask. "I've showed you some of my gifts. When will you show me yours?"

To my great surprise, Morgan laughed. "I suppose that's fair. Very well. Come here, Alexandria," she chuckled. Grinning from ear to ear, I stood up and streaked to her side. "Look there," she whispered, turning me to face the fireplace. Still holding onto my shoulders, she bent her head down to my level and stared intently at it. All of a sudden, flames appeared, crackling cheerfully as they ate at the wood. I gasped.

"You're pyrokinetic!"

Morgan chuckled at me. "I am."

"Can you teach me?"

She shook her head indulgently. "In time, Lex. In time."

I was learning that Morgan only used my nickname when she was willing to be closer to me. Instead of as my teacher only. This only seemed to happen when we were working with my powers. It excited her as much as it did me, to work with them, I think.

"Then teach me something else tonight? Something I haven't done before?" I pleaded. I could feel her hesitation and willed it to become a more positive feeling. Not for a moment did I think it actually worked. But soon enough, she was agreeing.

That night, I learned how to read auras. It was remembering what all of the colors meant that was all I had to worry about now. And it was the one time that Alyssa had no effect on my powers.

Chapter Twenty Nine

SECRETS AND SPELLS

I have to admit, after learning to use my powers, very little else mattered in my life. Schoolwork was boring. All of my classmates were irrelevant. And even spending time with my parents was becoming more of a chore than it should have been. I was hooked. Magick had sunk into my bloodstream, making everything else just a little less important.

But I was a Ryder and I persevered through all of my issues. I made sure to at least maintain a B average in my classes. Though I was getting a major A in gym due to all of my outdoor exercise. And I stuck through my piano lessons because to fail that was like failing at magick for me: unthinkable. I'd signed up for them, I'd wanted to learn, and I was going to get at least to the point of being decent on that thing.

More weeks passed and my powers were appearing more rapidly. In the middle of the school, I touched a wall and had images of children running through the halls thirty years ago. The kids at school began to feel more and more distant from myself. I'd stopped being a scandal and they just let me be. I was quite happy on that point.

Another few weeks passed. During that time, Morgan taught me rituals and ceremonies in preparation for Samhain. The day inched closer and the entire town was pulling out the pumpkins and the hay bales. Apparently it was an exciting event in Cedar Creek. I absolutely couldn't wait.

"There will be a full moon on Halloween this year! How often does that happen?" I heard a girl say on the bus. I smiled to myself, wondering what Morgan would have planned on such a powerful day. It seemed as if my thoughts were catching.

Nathan gave me a look that suggested that he knew I was spending that Friday night with

Morgan. I smiled slightly and looked out the window, watching trees trail by alongside the road. He knew I spent my weekends there. Most of those days I was the one to retrieve the mail from him. Or I would go with him to the grocery store and pick up what Morgan needed. Almost all of it was done in silence.

That night, I talked to my parents about Halloween. My dad always took me trick-or-treating, and I was still too young to use the age excuse. Good thing that the going door-to-door treat fest was well before dark in Cedar Creek. That would give me plenty of time to make it home and have my mom drive me over to Morgan's. (She'd taken to driving me since the days were getting shorter and the nights longer.)

I could feel the sadness even while unconscious. My psychic shields were weak while I slept, but they were still there. Which allowed me to feel Alyssa, though she couldn't take me back through time in my sleeping state. Despite the fact that my body needed rest, the sadness called to my consciousness in order to provoke a response.

Slowly, my eyes fluttered open in the dark room and I rolled over to look at my desk.

The rocking chair was back and Alyssa sat in it while staring at her hands again. I wasn't in the mood for the silent treatment. There was too much energy being expended already just in the shields to keep her out. I needed my sleep.

"Why are you so sad, Alyssa? Anger, frustration, and coldness I'm used to. Sad is a new one for you," I murmured into the air. She looked up at me, her eyes wide and imploring. Refusing to take the bait, I just raised my eyebrows at her, like Morgan did to me.

Nothing happened at first. Alyssa didn't move. She didn't speak. The only thing she did was continue to rock in the chair for a few more minutes. Finally, however, she faded away, chair and all. I sighed and went to lie back down, pulling the comforter up over my shoulder.

Suddenly, the north window burst open with a fierce wind! Leaves of all kinds blew into the room, including some ivy leaves that had been clinging precariously to the vine for the last few days. With eyes wide, I leapt out of bed and went to close the casements. As soon as I got them closed and latched, a vision hit me.

I stood outside the brick house beside a gothic-arched wooden door that looked older than any other part of the building. Ivy grew around it and I wondered instantly what it could be for.

Looking through another's eyes, I looked down at my tiny hands. Not Alyssa's hands, I noted. It was most likely the dark-haired girl I was seeing through, I decided.

Especially when I looked down at her right hand and found three keys. One was big and brass. The key to the attic. Another was of a similar size and bronze. It was this one that locked up the gothic door, I was sure. The last was small and golden. I had no idea what it was for.

The right hand closed over the keys, which were then placed into a pocket. Turning to face the door, the girl's hands both raised and I watched as the ivy quivered where it had been parted. In a voice just loud enough for the plants and magick to respond, she recited the spell.

"Hide my secrets, and hide them well.

Let none know I've cast this spell.
This secret is not meant to be shared.
Not one person shall be spared.
I call on thee to hide from me,
This door so that none shall see.
Close it up.
Make it disappear.
Let none find it.
Not even in under deepest fear.
So mote it be."

As soon as the words were said, the ivy burst with activity. New ivy leaves sprang up before the door, spreading across it until it could blend in with its siblings on the other side. Watching the door disappear from top to bottom, I couldn't help but think that it was a wound being stitched closed. And as soon as it was over, the ivy made it seem as if it never existed.

Nodding once to herself, the girl turned and walked away.

I gasped as I came back to my body. My head was reeling as I took in all that I had just seen. It was impossible. But it was true. Whoever the mystery girl was, she hid that door for a reason. She had taken the keys for a reason. There was something very serious going on here, and I needed to find out what it was.

For an hour, I stayed up wondering what I *could* possibly do. There was nothing. I was blank. I could go in search of the hidden door, except it was the middle of the night. There was also the fact that the key to open it was missing. Even if I did find it, it would be of no use to me. After running into a dead end for the third time in the hour, I sighed and finally went back to bed.

Chapter Thirty

SAMHAIN

"Thanks Mom," I said with a wide smile as we pulled up to the gate. She gave me a worried look.

My mom was always worried about leaving me here. But she felt better on the days she would see Morgan working in the garden.

"Be careful, Lex. Call me if you need anything and I'll come right back," she said as I gathered my sleeping bag and pillow.

I smiled widely at her. "Will do." When she didn't seem convinced, I leaned toward the front and kissed her on the cheek. "Love you, Mom. You can pick me up Sunday morning."

"Will do," she repeated with a roll of her eyes. Smiling impishly, I grabbed my things and climbed out of the car. I waited at the gate, waving to my mother as she drove away.

After she was gone, I opened the gate and carefully lifted my stuff over the salt line. Once it was on the path, I closed the gate and instantly felt like a metal door had just slammed home, creating an isolated room. It was the same feeling I got whenever I came to Morgan's now. The shield separating her world from the outer one was stronger than even I could have imagined.

"Lex," Morgan called from the bench.

Her face was bright with a wide smile. Morgan's icy eyes had deepened to a summer-sky blue, complete with a blazing glint that reminded me of the sun. She was possibly even more excited about today than I was. Which I thought was nearly impossible.

"Hello," I greeted in just as happy of a voice. Morgan tried to make her smile less friendly and more teacher-ish, but we both knew that she failed on that account.

"Come, let's put your stuff up. Then we can go." Following quickly, I dragged my sleeping bag into the house before setting it and my backpack in the corner beside the chest where I usually sat.

"Where are we going?"

"You shall see," Morgan said, sounding more like my teacher, but with the same warm smile as my friend.

Silently, knowing that she wouldn't reveal the surprise, I followed Morgan back outside. Slowly, we weaved our way through the garden until we came to the back of the house. Mostly vegetables were planted back here, so I was never around it much. Finally, our feet took us to the edge of the woods.

Morgan had taken me into the shady trees before. I wasn't scared. We'd often gone exploring for different plants that would test my knowledge. Now, as we stepped into the woods, I took note of the many bare branches. October's trees often began with fiery brilliance ... only to end in cold emptiness. That is how they were now. Bare and cold. They shivered with their own loneliness as they waited for winter to sink its claws deep into their bark. It was actually very sad.

For a long time, we wove through the trees, dead leaves crunching beneath our feet. As we walked, I couldn't help but notice that the sky was growing darker and darker. Dusk was approaching quickly and we still had not reached our destination. Still, I kept my thoughts to myself and trusted in Morgan's guidance.

I could tell the second we were nearing our journey's end. A force was pushing out against us, diminishing our good moods. I was wary now. The force sent wave after wave, like a pulse, out at us in a measuring sort of way. It wasn't a good feeling, having it wash over me like it was. But I knew that Morgan and I were headed for the center. Headed straight for the heart with this irregular beat.

The closer we got, the stronger the pulses. Finally, we came to a stop and I could feel a solid wall ahead of us. It was like the wall surrounding Morgan's land. This time, though, there was a slick, sliminess to the wall. Like moss coating a tree. It was an unpleasant feeling, to say the least.

With the light of the full moon, it was bright enough to see the ring of stones holding the wall in place. There was also a smaller ring of stones directly in the middle. The spot they enclosed was black where nothing ever grew. Scarred.

Stones led from the middle circle out to five

flat stones on the outer edges. It didn't take a guess to know that they formed a pentacle. The entire place thrummed with powerful energy, albeit while carrying a dark taint. So, when Morgan showed no fear and stepped over the outer wall, I followed slowly.

"We shall start with a simple Samhain ritual. To ask the Goddess for understanding and guidance in these changing times. And to give thanks for the harvests that shall preserve us through another year. To the Celts, this was the beginning of the year, this odd change of seasons when one year dies while giving promise of a new beginning," Morgan said in a low, low voice. I could only nod.

Suddenly, candles I hadn't noticed flared up on each of the pentagram rocks. White for spirit. Yellow for air. Red for fire. Blue for water. And green for earth. Each in the right position.

From there the ceremony proceeded.

After a few hours, our ceremony was concluded and our respects were made to Samhain and to the spirits. Looking at the sky, I realized that the moon hung almost directly over top of us now. Thinking that it was perhaps just as the sun, I wondered if it was almost midnight–the witching hour.

"Our respects are delivered. Now I would ask something of you, my dear Alexandria," Morgan said in a smooth, honey tone.

"What is it?"

"Have you ever been baptized as a child?" she asked, causing me to pull back my head in surprise.

"No. My parents are not religious."

Morgan nodded to herself. "I would like to perform a Wiccaning for you. It is mostly done on infants. But older children have also been through the ceremony. Will you let me perform the ritual?"

"Are you going to do anything like drown me?" My tone was cautious.

"No. I need only for you to lie in the circle, aligned to the stones," she said, pointing out the center circle. I was too curious to say no, of course.

I should have.

Chapter Thirty One

WICCANING

I lay down as directed. My head was aligned with the stones leading to the spirit candle, my left arm aligned to water, my left foot fire, my right foot earth, and my right arm air. After I was set, Morgan instructed me to close my eyes. I did as she asked.

Power seeped up through me, coated in that thick, slimy residue from the scar I was lying across. It made me uncomfortable to be there, but Morgan had her reasons. And as I lay there, I could feel her confidence and strength. No matter the scar, Morgan would protect me, I was sure.

Lying there, I heard Morgan's voice begin a low, soothing hum. The song she hummed sounded vaguely familiar, but I could not pinpoint where I had heard it before. In a matter of moments, her voice had switched from the ritualistic hum into a reedy chant in another language.

I knew she did this to empower the magick. Energy liked to be entertained, hence all of the tools in the Craft. Morgan also said that magick liked to be kept secret, instead of waved around. Which is why I was so right for the Craft. Because I wanted it to be kept a secret.

I felt something brush my forehead, then my wrists and ankles. It felt like strands of ribbon, but I wasn't sure. Morgan's voice began the familiar chant above my head and around my body. Finally, I heard the familiar words, "So mote it be."

Just as she said them, my eyes flew wide with a gasp.

I wasn't lying down on a blackened scar anymore. The full moon still hung above me, and the leaves were still fallen away. But it was close to winter. The air was frigid and cold.

I stood inside of the circle, my bare feet freezing against the cold ground. My clothing was from a dif-

ferent era. Maybe a few hundred years before my time. My shift was all I wore, and the wind pulled at that in a frighteningly purposeful way. I raised my head, feeling it brush my arms.

Glancing up, I could see my wrists bound above my head. My back was to a wooden stake. I gulped as I looked around me and watched as twelve women gathered bundles of sticks and piled them around my feet.

My heart pounded faster than ever and sweat beaded on my forehead. My eyes swiveled around the circle, looking for compassion, sympathy, or mercy in any of their eyes. There was nothing. They were as cold as the wind they had conjured to torment me. Fighting back tears, I glared straight into the crow-black eyes of the High Priestess.

Margarite. Oh how I hated her! The fury coursing through my veins was like nothing I had ever felt before. I tried to use it. I tried to pull at the power inside of me. But like my body, it was forever bound. I could not use it for harm. Not against the Coven. Not against my fellow humans, much less my fellow witches.

So I used it for something else.

Miles away, waiting for me in her grandmother's house, sat my daughter. She was waiting for me to come home to her. Or waiting to be retrieved by one of her twelve 'aunts'. My need to protect her was even stronger than the need I had to free myself. The last of my power and my energy went into cloaking her existence. I hid her from them. From the Coven. From even the villagers. They would not remember that I had a daughter. And after tonight, they would not remember me at all.

"You are so drained already, Mary?" Margarite taunted.

I lifted my sagging head to glare at her balefully. Had I any power left, I would have killed her. What they were about to do was exceedingly more terrible than exterminating an evil witch like her.

"You should not underestimate me. I have more virtues than you shall ever possess. The only reason she is making you do this is because I have power. Greater power than she could ever hope to attain," I announced to the rest of the Coven. They ignored me and continued to pile the wood for my death.

"Ah, but we will all attain it, dear Mary. With your death, the blood of traitors will be washed from our Coven and the magick will run pure for us once more."

"I have never betrayed my Coven," I snarled at her.

"You betrayed ME!" she screeched.

My head lifted and my nostrils flared, giving her the coldest and most disdainful look that I could manage. "You are not my Coven. You are an evil witch. And you deserve to burn."

Margarite's face cooled as she looked at me with those beady black eyes. "I have not brought harm unto another witch. You have. It is you who will burn." Her voice was quiet and even melodic as she said the words. "Light the fire."

As one, they began to hum a haunting melody. The tune carried through my head and I automatically wished to add my voice to theirs. The Coven's songs were ones of power and energy. They carried with them a weight that added to their wishes from the universe. Right now, they called on the power of fire to light my way into the spirit world.

I closed my eyes, feeling the energy coalesce into Margarite. They channeled their power through the will of the High Priestess. It was she who would be able to use the magick to bring about my death. I waited with my eyes closed, feeling the last kisses of the dying breeze.

I thought of my daughter. I remembered clearly her first steps. The first ceremony she joined with me *in. And I remembered the power that flowed through her very first breath. She would live. I would die. But she would always be protected.*

Then the fire started and all I could think of was the heat and flames. Behind my eyelids, the fire grew, orange colors dancing in my own eternal night. The smoke rolled upwards, smothering the air and choking my throat. Burning. I was burning! Madness flared up on my tongue and I opened my eyes as the last will of human survival urged me to find some way to escape. But there was no escape. I was burning!

Suddenly, the hem of my shift caught the blaze and it ate at my thigh. I screamed. I screamed and screamed and screamed. The fire ate away at me, bit by bit, and I could do naught but scream.

My throat was raw, I was screaming so loud. The pain. Oh, the pain! I hacked and coughed at the smoke that was no longer there while screaming over a pain that was no longer mine. My back was arched against it, while my ankles and wrists were held to the ground. My head, too, did not leave its position.

"Alexandria! Lex!" Morgan called my name

over and over again. I stopped screaming and my back settled back to the scar where a woman had died. Slowly, I peeled back my eyelids and glared accusingly at my mentor.

"What did you do to me?"

Chapter Thirty Two

RESTORED

Morgan didn't get a chance to answer.

As I opened my eyes, I could feel the power course through me. It was stronger than before. More alive. Freer. I wasn't held back. Not anymore.

While this feeling washed through me, I could feel my power seeping into the scar. I was grounding myself unintentionally. At the same time, I centered in a way that was almost too easy. It required no visualization on my part. I just ... was. Then there was the blissful clear-headedness that I had never truly achieved with all of my meditations.

I was one hundred percent focused. Which allowed the magick to seep from me and cause things to happen.

The candles lifted of their own accord. The earth on the outside of the outer circle trembled. Water rushed from a creek nearby to fill in the fissure I had created. Leaves fell out of the sky from a fierce wind I had called upon. Those were just the beginning.

My eyelids fluttered as I took in vision after vision. And the sensing of other things whether they be human, animal, living, or dead. I saw my mother in her office and I knew that it was happening right now, though it was past midnight. I saw Alyssa and the dark-haired girl playing with her harp. I saw the rocking chair being built from a single young tree and being delivered to the brick house covered in ivy. It flashed through my mind just as if I had been standing right there with them. As if I was a part of their time as well as mine.

Then I was out of my body, standing feet away, looking at Morgan and myself. Suddenly, I was back in my body. Out again. In. Out. In. Out. The last time, I tried to make myself stay and focus. But control was beyond me at that point.

Yet, perhaps what shocked me most was what I heard. Morgan's voice ... in my head. She was worrying about me. Scolding herself about the risks of this place. Then she thought something that really surprised me.

I had to try. The balance must be restored.

In my transcending state, it was clearer than it probably would have been otherwise.

What balance? I asked myself. I didn't realize the magick had sent it to her until she looked at me with wide eyes.

"My Goddess, Alexandria. Your power... What happened to you?" she whispered.

As she said the words, my hold on the magick disappeared. The candles fell with a thud, the flames flickering out as they rolled down the rocks and into the grass. The water seeped into the soil, leaving only the outer fissure as evidence of my tampering while the wind died down into a normal breeze. The visions slowed until I was receiving only one every few minutes.

"I wish I knew," I whispered back.

Despite my hold being lost, the power was still flowing through me. Still filling my body with a raw, untamed magick. It could be guided and coerced into doing my bidding, but I was insane if I thought that I could actually control it. I had the distinct feeling that that was most witches' mistake. You couldn't tame something so wild and free. It would break you before you got a real chance to try.

"What did you see, Alexandria? When I finished the Wiccaning, you saw something. What was it?" Morgan asked in a smooth tone that covered her inner turmoil well. If I wasn't twice the empath I was before coming here, I might never have noticed as she worked on containing her emotions.

"I burned at the stake." My voice was flat. Images flashed through my mind of hundreds of other women burning at the stake and I worked to shut them out. A nasty shiver ran up my spine as I tried to concentrate on Morgan alone.

"Ah. Mary." That was it. Nothing else. It was really getting on my nerves.

"What happened here, Morgan? The truth," I ordered for the first time ever. This power inside of me ... it had already changed me. Made me more willing to make demands. *Oh, that's going to be an issue.* "What is this place? And what about the balance?"

Morgan sighed and looked out over the

circle. The power seemed to pulse even more as she surveyed the land. She and it ... they were part of one another. Just like how it and I were now part of one another. *Why?*

"This has always been a place of power, Alexandria. A place of magick and spirits. In this place, the barrier is always lowered between the waking world and the spirit one. Magick flows across the barrier with free reign. And, sometimes, it will lock on a certain individual and inhabit them for the rest of their lives.

"The Native Americans of this region protected this place. They kept it safe from the white men coming to take their land. When they knew that they could no longer protect it, they chose to fight white men with the only allies they had: white women. They taught the female settlers how to respect mother nature. How to cultivate her knowledge and incorporate it into their own magick.

"Ever since, the Cedar Creek Coven has come here for all of their major rituals. But as these things go, it died out some time ago." Morgan looked back at me. At the scar.

"Why is it a part of you? Like it is a part of

me?"

"Because I was born here," she answered in almost a regal tone. My mouth dropped and my eyes grew round as saucers.

Suddenly, a flash showed me the dark-haired woman of before, lying inside of the inner circle, her stomach ballooned up. She was screaming and she was alone. Then there was the sound of a baby's cry.

"Oh my Goddess." When my eyes refocused, I couldn't help the odd look on my face as I looked at Morgan. "She was your mother. Alyssa's friend. She was your *mother*!" I shouted, leaping to my feet.

Morgan merely nodded. "Yes. And even my birth and Wiccaning in this place was not enough to restore the balance," she said calmly, trying to steer the conversation back.

"I want the truth, Morgan. The whole truth. What is going on here? How come you never told me about your mother? And what are you talking about? What balance?"

"Magick is neutral, Alexandria. Completely neutral. This place, when the Natives held it, was also completely neutral. When the witches got hold of it, the balance began to shift. Became more good than evil. Now goodness seeps into the things around it. It leaves a sort of mark after a time. Over the years, the mark grew into the protection surrounding this place.

"Now, after many years, the mark held and this land became as good as the witches using its power. But it was not the natural course this place should have taken. It should have stayed neutral.

"At the time of the witch trials, the High Priestess of the Coven ordered the woman who betrayed her to be put to death. They burned Mary Sullivan in this very place. A great evil was meant to wash away all of the good. But the mark still held.

"This place is tainted by what happened to Mary, but it is more tainted than it should be. Even the mark is tainted now. For generations, the witches in the area have tried to reverse the damage with ceremonies and Wiccanings. My mother was the only brave soul to believe that a birth of a child here would bring about enough good to restore the natural balance. Obviously, she was wrong.

"But your Wiccaning..." She let the sentence hang there.

As she said the words, I looked around instinctively. It didn't seem as if anything had changed. But there was a subtle difference. I reached out my consciousness to feel the shield. The sliminess was gone. That entire moss-like skin had disappeared. And it didn't feel particularly good, either. Yes. I had restored the balance.

Nodding to myself, I turned back to Morgan. "Now, tell me about your mother."

Chapter Thirty Three

TOOL

"No." Her answer was simple and firm. I tried to be as firm as her when I answered with, "Morgan."

"Alexandria Marie Ryder, do not take that tone with me. I will tell you nothing of my relatives. For the stories of that particular one, you will have to ask the house you live in."

"What does that mean?" I asked in confusion. "Use my psychometry on the house?"

Morgan nodded. "Use it on all that you touch, Alexandria. Everything that belonged to Alyssa. She wanted you to know her life. Ask the place where her life was spent."

"Why shouldn't I just ask her?" I questioned. Yet, I knew that I most definitely should *not* ask

Alyssa.

"Ghosts can twist the truth into a falsehood just as well as a living person can," was Morgan's grave response. I nodded.

"But the objects they touched hold only the truth," I finished in a murmur. It was like I was picking up on what she was going to say next. More intuition? Probably.

"Yes. Now, let us head back. It is well after midnight."

I nodded and felt myself get to my feet. Only, I was still sitting there. Turning, I could see myself looking up in shock at myself. My eyes were distant but I could still see out of them. Looking around at Morgan, I saw her wearing a small, wry smile.

"It appears we have more abilities to train tomorrow. Tell me, do you know what you are doing? Just take a guess, my dear," she said, her voice coated in amusement.

I looked again at my selves. One of me was sitting down, looking up at the other me. At the same time, I was looking down at myself, still sitting in the middle of the circle. Morgan was standing beside the circle, taking turns looking at each of us. Doing as Morgan suggested, I took a guess.

"I'm astral projecting, aren't I?"

"Yes, my dear Alexandria. It took me many years to learn that one," she said in a soothing voice. Suddenly, there were three Morgans standing before me. I blinked my astral eyes furiously. "And it should take you about a week to learn multiple projections. If I am correct in timing your power growth and control. Until this week is up, I must ask you to refrain from asking your house for the story. Start small. You can try the chair at the end of the week. Then you may move onto the larger conundrum if you so choose."

"Believe me, I will choose to," I said with a sarcastic smile.

"Since that is your wish, I suggest we get you rested up, my little witch. We begin just after dawn. Now, back into your body with ye," she said in a very grandmotherly voice. I smiled and nodded.

Closing my eyes, I focused on merging my two selves and concentrating on my five senses. Then, when I opened my eyes once more, I found myself sitting inside the circle with only one

Morgan beside me.

"That is a very useful skill," I murmured as I slowly got to my feet.

"Not as useful as you might think. Remember, Lex, magick is a tool to be used. Not a toy to flaunt about." Knowing she was about to add something just from calling me 'Lex' I waited while she smiled slyly at me. "Of course, it is a very fun tool to use."

"You will teach me tomorrow?" I asked with an unexpected yawn.

"Yes. Tomorrow."

We walked in silence back to her house where I was surprisingly tucked into Morgan's very own bed, instead of my sleeping bag on the floor. I was too tired to protest. My magick was energy incarnate, but my body was unused to so much power. I needed to rest my body if my mind was going to be able to continue using the magick born inside of me.

I woke to strange smells in the house. Flour and sugar. Cinnamon and chocolate. Then there was peanut butter and raspberry. Wiping sleepy seeds from my eyes, I sat up in Morgan's bed. Perhaps what was most odd was the music playing as I walked into the room. Morgan looked up at me and smiled.

"I knew you would be up soon," she said with a warm smile. She was being more my friend than my teacher today, I realized. After the balancing last night, I realized that my powers had grown almost to her level.

"How?"

"With an ability you shall learn today," she answered. I nodded and sat down on the chest, still listening to the music that was coming from nowhere that I could see.

"Morgan? Why did the circle suddenly balance last night and not when you were born?" I asked quietly. Was I edging too close to talking about her mother?

"Because your Wiccaning was good magick. A blessing. A natural birth and death are both neutral magick. They are a beginning and an end to life. A murder by magick is evil because it is a conscious desire to do wrong. My birth in that place does not alter the state it is already in. Though, now, a natural birth or death there would help to maintain the balance," she answered as she began pulling out mixing bowls and wooden spoons.

I nodded to myself, absorbing the knowledge she had given me. After a minute, I cocked my head to the side and watched her gather together food items on the counter. She even took out eggs and placed them beside the flour. I was thoroughly confused.

"What are you making?" I asked when I could no longer watch the bustle in silence.

"Me? Nothing," she answered with a sly smile. I felt a moment of apprehension before she said anything more. "You, however, are going to be baking."

"Me?" I asked warily, pointing at my small chest. Morgan nodded. "Why? And why so early?" I asked, looking to the windows. Okay, so it wasn't as early as I thought.

"It will help you practice your abilities. Come now, you have lots to do. There will be a bake sale at the town hall this evening for the high school to add more books to the library. Your mother will be fretting over having nothing to contribute."

"How do you know that?" I demanded in surprise. Morgan smiled. Suddenly, her eyes went out of focus and I could tell that she was *seeing* something. When she came back to herself, she looked at me.

"See for yourself," she offered.

I felt my lips pout out. When she only raised an eyebrow at me, I sighed. Closing my eyes, I felt my chords of power seeping into the earth, connecting with all of the living things as it stretched to the core of our mother. Then I began centering, losing myself into the colors around me. I blended with everything else in the universe like paints on a canvas.

"Alexandria!" Morgan's shocked gasp greeted me. I opened my eyes speculatively. She was staring at me with a piercing gaze. Then her eyes glared around the room before coming back to me. "What are you doing, child?" she asked gruffly.

"Centering," I answered, confused and a bit intimidated. Her brows pulled together as she refocused on me.

"What do you visualize as you center?"

"I imagine myself blending in with the

things around me. Bleeding into them like paint on a canvas. I run with the other colors. Why?"

"You've become invisible, dear child," she remarked in a much calmer voice. Gasping, I looked down to find that she was right. My body was completely gone! While I sat there in shock, Morgan's voice was filled with mirth as she said, "Well. That is certainly a useful tool, now isn't it?"

Chapter Thirty Four

BAKING

"What do I do now?" I complained as I stood with an apron on in the middle of the kitchen. For the record: baking a cake from scratch and *without* a recipe is a nightmare.

"What do you think you should do?" Morgan asked lazily from her chair where she was reading a book. The book of recipes sat beside her, so that she could be sure I was not peeking.

I thought about it, getting frustrated at my lack of intuition. It was the frustration that was bothering me. There was so much pressure to get this right, that it was hard to clear my mind. No matter my gifts, concentration was still key. One of many keys I was currently failing to find.

Clear your mind, Lex, I told myself.

After a few deep breaths, I turned back to the ingredients. A tablespoon of vanilla. That's what I needed next. Staring intently at the bottle of vanilla extracts, I concentrated on it and the measuring spoon I was using. With my mind only, I lifted the two objects and held them over the mixing bowl. Slowly, I tilted the bottle of vanilla until the liquid filled the spoon. Suddenly, I lost my hold on it and the spoon clattered into the mixing bowl while an unnecessary splash of vanilla was added before I tipped the bottle right side up and moved it to the counter. Then I groaned and covered my face with my hands.

"Separate the extra vanilla. You can do this, Alexandria. You have the talent. Just do what needs to be done."

I let out a deep sigh as my hands dropped. She was right. I had the power. I had the gifts. And I certainly had the stubbornness to keep going.

Before, as I'd worked, I'd tried forcing small amounts of the power to obey my will. Obviously that wasn't working. Taking another deep breath, I grounded and centered—while staying visible—before opening up to the power. The magick flowed through me, filling up my bloodstream and pulsing with each beat of my heart.

The music grew louder around me. The music that only I could hear. The music that had no source. And the same music I had heard Morgan humming during my Wiccaning. Somehow, this song was terribly important to whatever was happening to me. But I was not ready to know, yet.

The power flowed endlessly through me and I worked to mold it and use it as a tool. With a deep breath, I stretched it out to the spoon. It lifted effortlessly from the bowl and even rinsed itself off in the sink. Then I tried to pull out the extra vanilla from the mix. As though time were reversing itself, the vanilla extracted itself from the mix where it had sunk in already. Not a speck of flour or sugar was in the dark liquid. Feeling surprised, I guided it back into the bottle from whence it came.

"I did it!" I exclaimed, looking at Morgan with a wide smile.

She smiled back. "And what did you learn from this experience?"

"Magick can be guided, not forced."

"Well done. Now, what's next?" she asked, turning back to her book. I rolled my eyes and guided the eggs into cracking themselves before being added to the mixture.

For two cakes and three batches of cookies, I used my magick. The cakes and two batches of cookies were set aside for the bake sale. The last batch of cookies were for me and Morgan. Surprisingly, they didn't taste bad at all.

"So, what's next?" We'd worked on my intuition and telekinesis already. And after my invisibility act, I'd used my seer gifts to *see* what Morgan had seen about the bake sale and my mother having too much work in order to add to it.

"I believe, my dear, that it is almost time to call your mother. We don't want these goodies to go to waste."

I pouted the moment the words were out of her mouth. "But I have until tomorrow. I don't want to leave just yet," I complained. "Besides, tomorrow is *Dia de los Muertos*. There *has* to be a ceremony for that, too."

"My child, there is a reason I performed

your Wiccaning at midnight. You live in both worlds now, Lex. I fear that *every* day shall be *dia de los muertos* for you. Always remember that your first and most powerful skill will always be as a Medium between the worlds. This also helps you draw great power. For magick is nothing more than an in-between in itself. Always filling the space between fantasy and reality, possible and impossible, and holding itself between rational and irrational. That is what you are now, my dear girl. And that is also why you should call your mother today and not wait for tomorrow."

"Why?" I repeated, just as petulantly as before. Morgan smiled.

"Because, Medium or not, you are still just a girl. A girl who should spend time at home with her parents more days a week than she cares to admit," she said with an indulgent smile.

"Alright," I sighed in defeat.

I was just about to take a step toward the phone when I stopped myself. With a prideful smile at Morgan, I let myself step out of my body. Staring at my astral image, it was still hard to believe that I was literally in two places at once. I was in both minds and could pay almost equal attention in either body. It was tough, but manageable. I couldn't see how Morgan managed two astrals plus herself, though.

My brain followed my astral projection to the phone, since "she" was doing the most at the moment. Picking up the phone, I dialed my home phone number. It rang a few times before my mother picked up the phone.

"Ryder residence," her smooth voice said. She sounded tired. And stressed.

"Hey mom," I said with a bright smile and voice.

"Oh, Lex! How are you, baby? Everything okay at Morgan's?" she asked, her voice mellowing out a bit after she realized it was me.

"Yeah. Things are great over here. But I was wondering if you could come and pick me up today," I said in my best unconcerned tone.

"Um. Sure. But if things are going so great, why do you want to come home early?" She knew I wouldn't take that the wrong way. Which is why she said it as bluntly as my father would have. As I would have.

"Because, as Morgan said, we don't want all these treats to go to waste."

"What?"

"Morgan heard something about your bake sale for the high school. So we decided that some baking needed to be done."

"Well, aren't you thoughtful. I'll see you both when I get there. Love you, baby."

"Love you, too, Mom."

In the intervening time, Morgan and I set about straightening up—with neither of us physically handling a thing. True to her word, since I'd shown her what I could do, she equally produced her own feats of magick. Only when my mother pulled up did we leave the magick alone and set about doing very mundane things. Taking the goodies in hand, we set out through the garden and loaded them into the backseat.

My mom—one for all sorts of pleasantries—spent a few moments talking with my mentor. She asked if I'd been any trouble, thanked her for all the baked goods, and wished her well. I found it all amusing since I could tell that my mom, though nice to Morgan, really didn't mesh well with her. Perhaps it was just still that confusing to her why her nine-year-old daughter would prefer to spend time with this old woman instead of people her own age. Of course, Mom didn't realize that it was me she should be looking at weirdly.

Chapter Thirty Five

LULLABY

Before I knew it, I was back in my bedroom, changing into my pajamas. The day had gone by so fast once I was home. And every second alone that I had, I was using my magick. Practicing it. Honing it. Even in the shower, I tried to manipulate the water. It didn't work. Not because I didn't have the gift, but because elements were so much harder to work with than psychic powers.

As I made my way back to the bed, I was careful about two things in particular. One: my psychic shields. They were stronger than when I had left, creating thick, multiple layers that hugged my skin and shifted in consistency. Even Alyssa's sadness would not find a way through. My second worry was my psychometry. I could not use it yet.

Maybe on things not connected to Alyssa. But it would have to wait.

One week. That's all I needed. Then I could figure it all out. Silently, I slipped beneath the covers and drifted to sleep.

"Alyssa!" The melodic voice issuing from my mouth was not mine. My first thought was: Oh no, she's done it again.

"Victoria!" a brilliantly-smiling Alyssa exclaimed. She could be no older than six. Making me—Victoria— roughly the same age, I presumed.

"Girls. No need to yelp like wild dogs. If you're going to be causing such a ruckus, you best take it out of doors," said a maid who entered the room. My face twisted into an expression of contrite obedience. Alyssa rolled her eyes.

"Come sing with me, Victoria," Alyssa ordered, bounding the rest of the way down the stairs. Grabbing my hand, she dragged me into the familiar parlor where her piano sat.

"Alyssa," I groaned, "I can't sing."

"Yes, you can. Your voice is lovely." She was impossible to divert. Like a raging river that no dam could

hold. Unstoppable, unmovable, impenetrable Alyssa Rice.

"Sing that lullaby," she ordered as she took her place on the bench. I eased myself into a small chair beside the instrument. "You know. The one your mother sings to you," Alyssa continued.

I sighed. "Fine."

With a triumphant smile, petite little Alyssa began to allow her fingers to dance across the keys in the familiar melody. I closed my eyes and began to sing.

It was a simple lullaby, more with a unique tune than words. I sang it without any particular skill and was always glad to hear the piano override my own voice. That was where the true spirit of the song rested, after all.

Once the melody drifted to a close, I opened my eyes to look sheepishly at my friend. She was all smiles. It was worth it to sing for smiles such as those, though I was too self-conscious to do so in front of others. Alyssa knew it well and even encouraged me to keep to my natural temperament. Though, when her own desires willed it, she very much urged me to comply with her wishes.

Something changed in her expression a moment later. Rising off her bench, Alyssa came to stand before *me. Without any prompt that I could understand, she pulled me off my chair and hugged me tightly.*

"You're my best friend, Victoria. Always."

"You swear?"

"I swear."

The week passed in a long and dreadfully slow time. But pass it did. And as soon as it was up, I was back on Morgan's doorstep with my sleeping bag ready. This was the week. I would get my answers, starting tonight.

"You are sure you're ready for this?" Morgan asked that night.

I was standing with my arms and legs spread while she smudged me with a burning mixture of sage, cedar, tobacco, and sweet grass. She waved the smoke all around me before setting it on the table. It worked to purify me and cleanse my being. Next, she tied cedar into my hair, in order to protect me while I was on my spiritual journey. Of course I had to go alone.

"Yes. It is time I learned what is going on in my own house," I answered slowly.

"Then I shall let you go," she sighed and gestured to the door.

"Thank you for letting me do this, Morgan. I will be back as soon as I can." Just as I reached the door, a familiar black feline was waiting for me. "No. Even you cannot come this time. Some things must be done alone." Giving me one of those famous cat looks, the jade-eyed critter turned around and went to sit in the window until my return.

Waving, I left the small house and began my journey. It was the middle of the night, almost midnight, and I was heading back to the neutral place where I had spent Samhain. That seemed like the proper place to start.

Using my intuition, I found my way to the circle faster than I thought possible. I didn't even make it across the boundary before the past swallowed me.

"What is this place?" Alyssa asked me.

I smiled at my friend and turned to look at the witches gathering in their proper places. Five stood on the element rocks. One stood directly ahead of us clothed in white. Spirit. Looking to the right, the furthest from me, was a woman garbed in yellow for Air. Then there was Fire, clothed in bright red and orange. That girl was only sixteen. Next came Water, clothed in blue. Fire's twin served as Water. Last came Earth, clothed in deep green. She looked to be the mother of the other two elements.

Inside the circle, four others took the place of the directions. Each was garbed as the colors in a Native American medicine wheel. Black, white, yellow, and red. The skin colors of the races all bound together as it should be.

In the very center of the circle stood the High Priestess. My mother. Her ebony hair mixed too easily with her ceremonial black robes. Only her face and hands were distinguishable from the surrounding darkness.

Suddenly, my mother raised her voice and the entire Coven began to sing a haunting melody. It was the same song as my lullaby. Alyssa and I crouched in the shadows as we sat and watched the ceremony. I was in awe as I watched the magick taking place before my eyes.

Finally, the ceremony was ending and the witches were breaking apart one by one. No matter what magick they had performed, I could still feel the sickly feeling swimming inside of the barrier that kept intruders from this sacred place. They had not lessened it at all.

"Your mother is a spiritualist? Why have you never told me?" Alyssa demanded in her petulant seven-year-old voice.

"Not a spiritualist. A witch. And I wasn't allowed," I whispered back, pulling on her sleeve in the hopes that we would be able to slip away without getting caught. No such luck.

"Well, did you two enjoy the ceremony?" asked the twin garbed as Fire. Water stood beside her, a feathery eyebrow raised to study us. I sat, numb with fear, while they examined the two of us. Alyssa had no issues with it, however.

"Yes. How did you know we were here?" she demanded as if she were the one being spied upon.

"We have gifts, dear one. As do the two of you. We've been waiting for you to find your way to us," Water said with a knowing smile.

"Come. The others will be happy you are here," Fire stated and wove through the bushes toward the rest of the Coven. Water followed behind us so that we would not run for it. Not that Alyssa dared to think of that.

"Mother," Water called.

"We've found some young new witches. Should we train them or punish them?" Fire asked with a sly, mocking smile for us. I gulped.

"Witches?" Alyssa asked. "You want me to become a witch?"

"Only if you want to," Water said with a shrug that revealed she did not care either way. I stared at them with wide eyes.

Despite the fact that I had brought Alyssa to witness my mother's power, I felt betrayed. Becoming a witch was my future. It was the one thing that I was supposed to have. Magick was meant for me, not her. It wasn't right that Alyssa should have talent and fame as well as magick, too.

Slowly, my envy for my friend hardened into a small ball in my stomach. I tried to let go of it. Alyssa was a good friend to me and I would try to be a great friend to her, as well. I had to get over my fool jealousy and let her share this experience with me.

All too soon, it was settled. Alyssa and I would both be trained to use our young gifts. It would be harder for Alyssa to learn, considering her parents' involvement in her life. But with my help, she would stay current with the lessons. Everyone was counting on me to help her. So I would try.

Chapter Thirty Six

POTENTIAL

I pulled back into myself as the memory dissipated before my eyes. The waning moon still threw a great deal of light across the circle, unlike in the memory. Stepping over the barrier, I found myself swallowed into yet another memory.

"Victoria, focus." Anne scowled, snapping her fingers in my face. I snapped to attention.

"Sorry. I was just watching..." I didn't need to finish. She knew who I was watching.

"Alice and Alyssa are working just as hard as you and I. There's no need to play governess," Anne stated.

I let my eyes drift from my lap back up across the circle to where the other two girls were sitting. Anne—

Water—was my mentor now. She helped me to learn the Craft while her twin, Alice—Fire—was set to tutor Alyssa. It was broad daylight and Alyssa and I had lied to her parents, saying that we were just going to my house to work in the garden. My mother would inform us if we were close to getting caught.

"Focus, Victoria. You'll be falling behind soon," she admonished. The comment stung as I folded further in on myself.

"She seems to be doing well," I said in a tightly controlled voice as I watched my friend.

Only then did Anne become slightly distracted with Alyssa's progress as well. "Yes. It was a surprise to us, being able to receive her. She has so much raw potential. And even magick seems to have trouble disobeying her force of will," she added with a teasing smile.

"Yes." My voice was glum and I could not change it.

Anne looked at me with a knowing expression. "You're filled with more power and determination than you realize, Victoria. But your styles of using it are vastly different. She is like fire, pouring out her passion and will until it covers acres of land. You are like water, flowing your power into the best choices and *uses. Ultimately, you can keep the fire in check. All you have to do is embrace and guide your new abilities. Let us start again."*

I drew in a deep breath as I came back into myself once more. Whatever was happening between Alyssa and Victoria, it was turning for the worse. Victoria's jealousy was taking hold of her, though she tried to fight it. Strangely, I was more afraid of being in Victoria's head now than I was of being in Alyssa's. What could she have done in a fit of jealous rage? I was too frightened to find out.

Find out I must, however. Another few steps brought me to almost the center circle. Here, the past grasped me once more.

"Stay by me, Alyssa," Alice whispered to me. I smiled up at her and nodded my head.

Alice was like me. We could control the flow of magick better than the others. The power knew better than to make a battle of wills between the two of us. We could fight it until we won.

Not like Anne and Victoria. They placated the magick. They couldn't control it. They allowed it to control them. Like a river that only went where the land guided it, following the curves of soil and ridges. Followers. That was all.

I was like fire, though. I created my own path, even if it meant destroying the things standing in my way. Nothing could hold me back. I was strong and determined and had astounding potential in all that I did. Especially magick.

The ceremony was about to begin. It was the first Victoria and I would join in. There were three other girls involved, but I didn't bother to learn their names. They were weak compared to me, and even compared to Victoria. In their lifetimes, they would be accomplished if they learned to scry. Something Victoria and I had both mastered only a few days ago.

"Positions, young witches," Catherine called to her twin daughters and the apprentices, including myself. Together, the four of us gathered by the stones marked for water and fire.

As we began the ceremony, voices lifted into a wordless melody. It was not the lullaby Victoria and I were most used to. Rather, it was deeper and more res-onate. It was a song of the earth itself. My bones tingled *and my fingers twitched as though I were playing the melody on the piano. Power coursed through me as I felt my eyes close and give myself over to the power of the music. Nothing else in the world could have influenced me so much in my entire life.*

I felt as if liquid gold were burning through my bloodstream. Power so fierce and full of intent. As the music controlled me, I felt for the first time what it was to be a grain of sand caught in a windstorm. I had no control in this situation.

All at once, the power let loose! Around me the ground shook and rumbled and the force field surrounding the stones vibrated like a tuning fork. The music exploded out from me in crashing waves of energy. This feeling was like nothing I had ever felt before. I was absolutely consumed with the power.

My own power coursed through me in torrential waves as I came out of the memory. I gasped as similar tremors shot through the ground and rippled through the newly balanced shield. Unlike Alyssa, however, I was not consumed. I tempered the magick even while it continued to blast forth from me and affect the things around me. My control was even greater than Alyssa's. Even if she was only seven...

Something had happened to Alyssa. It must have. That power was going straight to her head. It was like watching a movie I'd already seen: I just knew what happened next. My stomach twisted as I got caught up in a different story than the one I had imagined existed.

But in order to get the full story, I had to continue. And the circle had only one more memory to show me.

"Alyssa? Alyssa Rice? Wake up child!" an old voice croaked beside me. My head moved and I heard collective sighs of relief. Blinking, I opened my eyes to view the Coven surrounding me in apparent concern.

"What happened?"

My body felt drained and lifeless. Memories started to seep back and I began to panic. Had I lost my magick? Reaching for it, I felt something inside of me. Slowly and carefully, I opened my mind to it. Suddenly it all rushed back and I sighed in relief.

"The music got to you. Your power was triggered by it, creating quite an effect," Victoria answered

without inflection. It was like she didn't care.

"Victoria! You've never felt such power before. To be carried away so completely..."

"Alyssa," the old crone beside me admonished.

I looked at her with wide eyes. "It was the music," I said in a low voice. "It was just so beautiful and I couldn't control it." I could see the change in her eyes. She was falling for my manipulation.

"Then it's best that you learn to control it," Victoria's cold voice said into the silence. My head snapped over to glare briefly at her. What was she trying to do to me?

"I quite agree," said her mother, the High Priestess. "Alyssa, you are not to have anything to do with these songs except for when you are here amongst us. Is that understood?"

My mouth opened as I stared at her indignantly. They expected me to have nothing to do with the most beautiful music I had ever heard? Were they mad? How could I just walk away from something so exotic and lovely? But the looks on their faces said that I had to. One way or the other, I had to give up something.

"Understood," I muttered sullenly.

Chapter Thirty Seven

ROCKING CHAIR

My walk back to Morgan's was not done alone. Almost as soon as I stepped outside of the barrier, the familiar cat stood by to guide me home. Which was a good thing, since I had barely enough energy to make it back. Tomorrow, I would begin my search for the truth once more. At Morgan's house, I was never ambushed in my sleep.

Following a black cat in the middle of a forest probably wasn't the brightest of ideas, but I had no problem keeping right behind her. Together, we wove through the forest until we made it to the garden. Once there, the path led me straight to the door. Thank Goddess Morgan knew I was coming. I doubted I had strength left to knock.

"My dear child," she whispered, pulling me inside. "Let's get you to bed."

Like the night of my Wiccaning, I was too tired to protest when Morgan tucked me into her own bed. I was asleep long before she turned out the light.

"Good morning, Alexandria," Morgan said in a low voice as I emerged from the bedroom. I was wiping the sleepy seeds from my eyes while trying to stifle a yawn at the same time.

"Good morning," I murmured back.

"Did you sleep well?" she asked, setting a plate of eggs, bacon and toast on the table for me.

"Yes. Thank you. For everything," I added. Morgan merely nodded and sat beside me with her own plate.

It was funny to watch her. She was so curious as to what I found, but I knew she was trying to keep herself from asking questions. For about a minute I reveled in the fact that I knew something she didn't know. Then my own curiosity overrode everything else.

"I saw through Victoria's eyes and Alyssa's

this time. I saw how they began as young witch-es. And I also saw what Alyssa's power could do. Why does she react like that to music?"

Slowly I ate as Morgan and I both pondered our nights. I wanted to tell her everything, but I didn't have the full story yet. There were pieces of the puzzle that were still hidden. And I knew that I would have to keep going in order to find the truth. The honest, real truth. Something I could only learn from their objects. Silently, my head turned toward the dreaded rocking chair. It was next.

"Perhaps for the same reason you react to the circle—it is in your spirit. Your soul. Music is like that for Alyssa. The weather is like that for me. Each thing seeps into our bones and triggers something inside each of us. Music for Alyssa. Stones for you. Weather for me."

"Stones? I thought you just said it was the circle?" I demanded. Morgan smiled.

"A circle of stones. The first time your magick was triggered, that I know of, was when you came to my house and touched the gargoyles. Is there another source, then, for your power?"

I was ready to agree with her. Tell her that

it must have been the gargoyles. But a part of me knew it was wrong. Suddenly, the image of a single green leaf fluttered through my head and I knew instantly where my power originated.

"Yes. There was another source. I got it from the ivy. All along, it has been the ivy that unbound my powers and set them free."

"Ah. Then that would explain the tendril on the bench. It appeared the same day you first wandered into my garden, I believe."

"Yeah..." The image reappeared in my head of the single tendril of the vine winding around the bench. An awkward silence fell and I took that time to finish my food before looking at the chair.

"You will try again so soon?" Morgan asked quietly as she lifted our plates to the sink. Looking back at her, I nodded.

"I have to. I need to know."

"Then go ahead. I will wait patiently for my answers until this story has played out in full," she answered. I smiled thankfully at her and hugged her around the waist. Tearing myself away from my mentor, I sighed and took a step toward the chair.

In all honesty, it didn't look very intimidating. Neither did Alyssa or Victoria, though. Looks were deceiving. And the wooden, elegant rocking chair looked like nothing more than an old antique. Yet, it felt like so much more.

An aura of its own exuded from the chair. There was a past to it that few people knew about. It contained strain and pressure; glory and triumph; tears and laughs; and a dead little girl's memories. Soon, I would merge my memories into it as well.

Well, here goes nothing, Lex, I thought to myself. With a deep breath, I took the last step forward and turned to sit in Alyssa's rocking chair.

"You're playing with fire, Alyssa. I should have never taken you to the ritual," Victoria hissed.

Once more, I saw the attic from outside of their minds. Alyssa was sitting in the rocking chair, staring condescendingly at a fretting Victoria. They looked to be eight. Maybe nine.

I gulped.

"I am playing with fire? No. I am controlling fire. I am creating my own path. You, however, are

drowning. You flounder about in your pool of repressed magic. You're too afraid to embrace it. You cower before the ocean at your feet and you refuse to touch it. Your problem, Victoria, is that you're jealous that I embrace my magick. And I grow stronger and freer by the day. Soon enough, I won't need your precious coven and I can become a solitary witch."

My mouth dropped at the same time that Victoria's did. How could Alyssa say those things? Stunned beyond all comprehension, I barely noticed when Victoria's eyes filled with tears. Suddenly, they were pushed back roughly and her jaw strained as she clenched her teeth. Her pretty eyes were suddenly cold and distant.

"You'll be nine in a month. You really believe that you will be ready for solitary work in so little time? As a nine-year-old, myself, I can assure you that there is a definite increase in ability. You are still lacking in skill, however. It will take more than a few months for you to learn that, Alyssa." Even her voice was cold.

"Maybe for you, Victoria. But I have talents you have yet to possess. I will be ready when the time comes."

For a moment, all was still and silent. Alyssa sat in her rocking chair as though it were a throne. Victoria stood in quiet determination. Their eyes blazed off one another, ready to ignite sparks in the air. Finally,

Victoria spun on her heel and made her way to the stairs. There, she paused and glanced chillingly over her shoulder at Alyssa.

"As will I, Alyssa. As will I."

"She's just jealous," Alyssa murmured to herself.

I sighed on the inside, knowing I was back in her head. Someplace that had truly become disgusting to me. Slick like the oil film that had been a part of the barrier in her time. It seemed to have leaked into her very soul and now I had to suffer with it.

"Victoria doesn't know what it's like to have this much power," I whispered again.

Standing, I trailed over to the harp that was immensely taller than myself. Someday I would grow into its size. But I didn't want to wait that long.

Plucking at the strings, I imagined myself taller, older, more beautiful. I pulled more at the strings. Music drifted into the air and I closed my eyes. Magic flowed through my veins and I plucked even more vigorously on the strings, coaxing the magic from their endless notes.

So absorbed was I that I didn't even notice the change. I hadn't yet realized my fingers had lengthened and my posture was bent more as I pulled at the sections of the strings my eight—almost nine—year old hands were used to. Instinctively, my fingers trailed upwards, allowing me to relax, and added a texture to the music that sent it into a state of ascendance such as I had never heard before.

But it was only an illusion. As soon as I opened my eyes, nothing had changed. It was merely a trick of the mind, making me believe I had actually changed my body. My goal through life had finally been accomplished.... Only in my mind. I almost burst into tears of frustration right there.

Yet, I could not. If I was to accomplish my wishes of opening to my full potential in a much shorter time frame, I could not cry. Instead, there was nothing for it but to keep trying and practicing my magic. Nothing would stand in my way. Nothing.

Chapter Thirty Eight

FORMS OF BETRAYAL

Gasping, the room in Morgan's house came back into focus. I blinked several times as the fire danced before me. The clock on the mantel read eleven thirty and I was surprised that it hadn't been that long since I started. Too soon, I would have to leave her house and head for my own. Endings always seemed to be in the same place where they began.

Yet, the chair had one more memory to show me. One more sinister experience from the minds of nine-year-old girls. The kind that caused shivers to run down my spine.

I wasn't in either of their heads, this time. Instead, I

stood about where my bathroom began in my room. It was beside Alyssa's desk. Dimly, I wondered why she had moved the chair to her bedroom.

Everything looked the same as before. Including an ivory-clothed Alyssa sitting calmly in her chair with the too-familiar dress hanging to her knees. Again, her ankles were crossed and she had her eyes on her hands in her lap. Victoria stood right about where I had been the first time I saw Alyssa sitting like that. I remembered fainting when she looked up into my eyes.

Slowly, as if I couldn't help myself, my feet carried me right up to where Victoria stood. Her eyes blazed as she glared at Alyssa. As before, Alyssa's features were blank. Expressionless. Unreadable. She was giving nothing away to her rival.

Then she looked up and her eyes bored into Victoria's the way they had bored into mine. Thank Goddess that memories were different from real life experiences. There was no chance of me fainting this time.

"What do you want, Victoria?" Alyssa's voice was as chilled as ice.

"You know, they kill witches who betray their covens." I was shocked at the even colder tone that Victoria used. Glaciers and polar ice caps could not be colder.

"I have no coven, Victoria. I betrayed no one."

"You used your power for evil, Alyssa. The most heinous evil. If that is not betrayal, then tell me what is."

Alyssa's eyes suddenly burned with fire as she stared up at Victoria. "Betrayal is when the person who is supposed to be your best friend decides that she no longer wants anything to do with you once she realizes she's not as powerful."

"You think I am jealous of you, Alyssa?"

"Yes."

"You're wrong. I pity you," Victoria said in a silky, persuasive, cruel voice. It was a side to Victoria I had never seen before in all of the memories.

"You're the one that deserves pity!" Alyssa spat.

"No. I don't have to be perfect for my parents to love me. And I don't have to be the most powerful in order to love myself. Perfect love and perfect trust, Alyssa. That is what you get when you enter a coven as you should. You can't handle that. And that's why you deserve my pity."

Tremors shot through the air, blurring the world inside of the bedroom. Almost instantly, a force built around the bedroom in order to contain them. The tremors came from Alyssa. The block from Victoria.

Alyssa glared viciously.

"We'll take this to the attic," she snarled.

"Lead the way," Victoria offered, holding out her hand. Almost instantly, Alyssa vanished from view. Seconds later, Victoria followed suit.

They were using a glamour to make themselves invisible. That was how they'd gotten around the house without anyone noticing Alyssa's whereabouts. My thoughts rested on this as I came out of the memory. The two had used magick to slip up to the attic. It had ended there. Something had happened there that ended in Alyssa's demise.

It was as I was sitting in that used-to-be-formidable rocking chair that I realized that the next step would take me home. I needed to be in the attic to get the last piece of my puzzle. The next piece, however, resided in the piano.

"Are you ready for lunch?" Morgan asked, breaking into my thoughts.

"Yes, please."

Leaping from the chair, I rushed to sit at the table where a plate of food awaited me. My magick was already draining me some. I needed food and a resting period before I went home. That would be time enough with Morgan. It had to be.

"I have to go home for the rest of the story," I informed her.

"I know. What will talk to you next?"

"The piano. Then something in the attic. Probably her harp. I think Alyssa loved that more than the piano. That's why it's in the attic—so she doesn't have to share that music with anyone else. I think it's how she got her power. Alyssa didn't follow the rules," I informed my mentor as I continued to eat.

"You will tell me the story when you have finished this journey?"

"Absolutely," I promised. It included her mother. She had a right to know.

After another half an hour, I was ready to leave. I'd washed my own dishes and helped Morgan to straighten up the house. Then I called my mother and asked her to pick me up. So, with a curiosity burning inside of me, I headed out the door.

As soon as my hand touched the handle, I was sucked back into Victoria's mind.

"She betrayed us!" an older witch screamed. My mother looked at her with sad eyes.

"Alyssa is just a child, Nadia. She doesn't know that what she has done is betrayal." Mother's pleas were not taken seriously by anyone. Least of all me.

"How could she not? What she has done has gone far beyond the laws of the Coven. They are crimes against humanity itself," Elizabeth, my father's sister, replied coolly.

"Alice was to teach her the rules of the Coven. Instead, she taught her only her own selfish desires," Patty sniffed.

Instantly, Catherine was on her feet. "Don't you go accusing my daughter of twisting minds! Alyssa came into the circle with a hole for a heart. Alice tried to warn you but you wouldn't listen. Now the girl has betrayed us and you want to blame my daughter?"

"Well I don't see anyone else here able to twist minds like your daughter is able. Obviously she passed this particular gift of hers to Alyssa Rice," Nadia sniffed.

The fighting continued. Each member of the Coven picking apart at the other. My whole world was falling apart and even my mother couldn't put it right again. Alyssa had knowingly betrayed us all. Now she was *tearing us apart.*

Alyssa was destructive. Too destructive. I'd known it for years but had not the courage to do anything about it. But now, I didn't have a choice. Something had to be done. And I was the only one who could do it.

Standing in the doorway all this time, I finally eased open the aged wood and slipped outside.

There were many forms of betrayal. Betrayal of friends. Comrades. Even life. Alyssa had done all of these things. She had truly broken them and scattered them to the wind. Morgan had told me how the Coven had split when her mother was just a girl. It made sense now. And no matter what Victoria had done to rectify the situation, nothing could cure it.

Chapter Thirty Nine

MUSIC

"You alright, honey?" my mom asked me again for the tenth time.

"Just tired," I replied. It was true and she could see it in my face whenever I looked at her. The interrogation hadn't stopped since we left Morgan's.

"Maybe when we get home you should go lie down," she suggested yet again.

"Nah. I'll be fine. I was actually going to practice on the piano for a little while, if you don't mind."

Her expression was skeptical but her answer was reassuring. "No, I don't mind."

For a minute, I wished she had minded. To go from one twisted scene to the other was draining. Emotionally and physically. The pieces didn't fit in order and I had to scramble around to try and make sense of the thoughts and images flittering through my brain. If my mother had just said I couldn't play, then I might have had time to sort through it all. But I knew that once I had started, there would be time for nothing but Alyssa, Victoria, and the secret hidden beneath the ivy.

When we arrived home, I took my things up to my room and headed down to the piano. Mom was back in the office, which left enough walls between us to where she might not be bothered by the music. And she might not notice if the music started getting ... odd.

Slowly, I inched toward the polished grand piano. The music sheets waited on their stand and the ivory keys almost looked inviting. Too bad I knew what was going to happen the second I sat down. Now, all I could feel was apprehension ... and fear.

Sitting gingerly on the stool, I rotated and placed my fingers on the starting keys that I had learned. As soon as the cool ivory touched my skin, the mist rolled in over my eyes and I was taken back to the past.

It's not right! *I bit my lip as I poured over the sheets on the stool beside me. It wasn't there. The magic didn't come to life with the music. Taking my pencil, I added a few more notes, rearranging some already on the page, and erasing entire ones altogether.*

Satisfied for the moment, I placed the sheet up on the stand and let my fingers flow across the keys. At first, there was nothing. Average music. Nothing magical. And then I hit one spot and I instantly filled with flowing power. The sweet, heavenly feel of it soaked into my skin before another average note tore it away.

Instead of tearing the sheet down and trying to rework it again, I took a deep breath and stood up to walk. I paced around the room a few times before a glance out the window showed me Victoria coming up the walk. I smiled in relief as I saw my friend. Even if she didn't look happy, I knew that seeing her would help me get the music done.

"Victoria!" I exclaimed in greeting as I threw open the front door. She smiled slightly at me.

"Alyssa." Her voice wasn't happy. She wasn't happy. Worst of all: she was glowing with power. A stab of unease shot through me as I processed her strength.

Should she ever learn how to use it, *I will be the weak one. The thought made me sick. To be weak compared to Victoria was a step back, not a leap forward.*

"I could feel you practicing from my house," my friend informed me.

I didn't know how to take that. Did that mean I was so powerful that a witch over a mile away could feel me? Or did it mean that she was so powerful, her senses stretched out that far? The questions ate me up inside.

"You're lucky my mother didn't notice. She'd string you up for touching the music outside of ritual and on your own."

"Is that why you've come?" my voice had a chill to it. Victoria nodded.

"Yes. With me here, at least, you're still 'amongst us' and can continue practicing." There was another reason, I was sure. But she was technically right. And if the Coven was disturbed by it, then I still had her to fall back on. A true friend.

"Thank you, Victoria," I replied, forcing warmth and gratitude into my tone.

"You're welcome. I'm going to go sit down for a while," Victoria added, yawning widely. It was the first time I noticed that it wasn't unhappiness that had hold of her. It was fatigue.

"You were up practicing all night?" I demanded.

Victoria nodded, yawning again. "Anne took me to the circle. She thinks that if I work hard enough, practice more, that I could help her in the next ritual. The full moon is only a week away."

"Really?" My voice was carefully neutral. Alice wouldn't let me join a rite yet. She said I had too much spirit and not enough temperance. But Victoria was almost ready? I almost spat, I was so angry!

Victoria nodded again. "I have the solemnity to progress well, she says. But I lack the confidence in my own abilities. It's what we've been working on for weeks now. It's like I can feel the power. But it's just the other side of a waterfall and I can't seem to take the plunge. I stay in the safe currents without allowing myself to dive deeper. Anne keeps trying to push me further, but in the end, it is I who must jump."

"You don't think of magic as fun. It's holding you back," I announced.

Victoria shook her head. "I think of magic as the responsibility that it is. It keeps me guarded against reckless misuse of our gifts." There was no doubt that there was judgment in her tone.

"Well, you lie on the settee for a while, and I shall play." Victoria nodded and moved to the proffered

seating. Stretching out her tanned legs, she was asleep almost before I'd made it back to the piano.

Seating myself, I set aside my project for a while and played the lullaby we knew best. Suddenly, the ending flowed into something else. Something sweet and beautiful that sang with power. It was rich and fulfilling, making my blood rush with adrenaline. On and on it played, having a life of its own. I could barely handle the flood and the rush of power. Clinging to it with my fingertips, I found myself drowning in indescribable pleasure.

Finally, the music drifted to a close, taking the magic with it. I almost wept for the loss of its absolute bliss. And as soon as the final note hung teasingly in the air, I ripped apart my overused sheet and wrote out the notes and cadences of my astounding music.

The whiteness faded from my eyes, taking Alyssa and her music with it. Without thought—I was still lost in the past—my fingers moved along the keys, repeating the notes. This time, it was me and not Alyssa playing the piano. I was trying by memory as my own power tingled in my fingertips and begged for a release. And though I was sure there were mistakes, my music sounded similar to hers. But I got nothing from it.

Alyssa did, however. The air drew toward me, eager for what I was offering. And if my psychic shields weren't up, I was sure Alyssa would force the music from me once more. I almost invited it, just to finish this. But losing Alyssa to the music would never ensure I got to hear the rest of the story any time soon.

"Give me the last one, Alyssa. Show me what this music did to you," I whispered so low that no living creature could possibly make out the words.

My curls swung as my mother twisted my face to add color to my lips. The golden ornament dug into my scalp and the lace of the sleeves caused my arms to itch. Black shoes hugged my feet almost too tightly while my dress put a severe limit on my breathing. And yet, for all of the discomforts, I'd never felt so grown and accomplished.

"Hurry, Mother. I'm next," I hissed as the violinist was closing up his piece.

Adding the last bit, my mother grasped my hand

and whispered, "Good luck, sweetheart. Make me proud." The pressure increased tenfold.

In a matter of seconds, my name was called and I was striding out with a confident gait not common in nine-year-olds. Especially not nine-year-olds faced against a plethora of imaginative, fantastic musicians. But I had something those other musicians couldn't imagine on my side. Magic. It provided a perfect insurance against any failings. And any usurpers to my rightful place.

I sat at the piano and placed my fingers lightly on the keys. Closing my eyes, I pressed the first reverberating note. My magic spiked. The second key was struck, and my power held steady. Then it flowed. The magic and the music held sway over the enthralled crowd. It played through their minds, swaying me in their favor. Each pitch and note made me the clear victor. And as the song drifted over them, my position and esteem were already well-established.

Nothing could be left to chance, however. Even as the music turned over in the minds of those whose judgment would decide all, it laced through the air to my fellow competitors as well. Those of inferior ability were passed over easily. Of those who served to challenge me in the eyes of others, something must be done.

The magic seeped into their skin. Their hearts. Lungs. Absorbed into every inch of their bodies, it took root in their souls. Like poison, the intent was lethally clear.

Just as sudden as my attack, a power exploded throughout the room, halting it almost before it had begun. My hands moved mechanically as my eyes shot up to search the crowd. Victoria wasn't even looking at me, so concentrated on her efforts as she was. Fury erupted in my chest as she extinguished my magic. When she had finished, it was as if nothing of my power existed.

With a heart grown cold with fear and rage, I redoubled the spell in my song upon its closing. Though I had failed in neutralizing my competitors—a fact which Victoria would pay most severely for—I would still succeed in winning the competition. The judges were given no choice.

No one thought I could win. Not a nine-year-old girl against hundreds of the world's greatest classical musicians. I was a charming side-attraction for the sponsors to point at and hold out as a testament for other children to learn this trade. But they'd never expected me to take home the trophy. And yet...

I did.

Chapter Forty

CALLING THUNDER

I had one place to go for the rest of the story. One place where all things would come to an end. Where all the answers would be laid bare. The attic.

My feet led me up the stairs before I'd even finished the conscious thought. I paused at the attic door to pull the key out of my pocket. I didn't get a vision from the action. I wouldn't get one until I reached the actual attic, I knew. So, when I entered the dark space, I turned and closed the door. Then I took the snow globe and twisted the little knob on the bottom before setting it down on the stairs. Just as Alyssa had done.

Slowly, I took each wooden step under my feet and worked my way to the top of the stairs.

Was I anxious for my answers? Absolutely. Was I dreading them? More than I could possibly say.

A full moon shone through the windows of the attic. Alyssa sat on the aged wooden floor, a chalk circle surrounding her. There was no altar to do magick on. She didn't need one, apparently. Instead, four stone chalices marked the directions and the elements. The north was filled with black earth from the garden. East was holding incense, the smoke curling through the air. South held a burning candle, the flame dancing with the element of fire. The last chalice in the west held water.

Alyssa sat with her eyes closed, facing the southern window where the moonlight shone brightest. It lit up the workings of magick better than a light bulb possibly could. All around her, the air shimmered. It twisted and changed, dancing with fey lights.

The words Alyssa was murmuring began to go faster, flying from her mouth and causing the elements to move unnaturally. Suddenly, the hairs on my arms began to stand. Power coalesced around me and I knew that it was practically choking Alyssa. She had called down the thunder, and was getting the lightning, too.

I knew what she was trying to do. She was trying to perform her Rite of Ascension. Alone. With no guidance, no Coven, and no protection. Alyssa was opening a one-way door to a world that she was not ready for. It could only end in disaster.

I don't know what happened to end the ritual. All I knew was that it had not succeeded. My last sight was a white flash and I'd felt a tremor before returning to my time. My house. My dark attic. My dusty footprints on the floorboards.

Yet, it didn't feel like my place at all. Alyssa still roamed here. This was still her turf. And it was feeling less and less welcoming the more I learned the truth about the little girl I had wanted to help not so long ago.

I took a deep breath and stepped farther into the shadowed room. My gaze immediately sought out Alyssa's circle. It was still there. Not chalk, anymore, but a blackened scar. Whatever had happened had burned the circle straight into the floor. And yet, it hadn't touched anything else. Gulping, I looked away from it.

As before, my eyes sought out the harp. It

was Alyssa's favorite object. And I knew that it, at least, had something to tell me of Alyssa Rice. Inching slowly forward, I reached out a finger and touched one of the cold strings.

Her hands ran over the strings as her head bowed and her eyes closed. Faster and faster her fingers blurred over the instrument's chords. A bright melody filled the air and I wondered how much magick Alyssa was drinking in from it.

Suddenly, different music drifted up from the stairs, cutting off Alyssa's concert in an instant. Her eyes bored into the space where whoever it was would appear. My eyes flashed between Alyssa and the top of the stairs, waiting for someone to make their way into the dragon's lair.

Alice stalked into the attic, her mouth pressed into a thin line. I watched as Alyssa's eyes widened. Then, as only Alyssa was able, she stood regally, smoothing out the blue dress I had seen from before and laced her fingers in front of her. The look she gave Alice was polite and calm. Not at all like the Alyssa faced with Victoria. Victoria unsettled her. Alice did not.

"Hello, Alice. Did you need me for something?"

"It's forbidden for you to use music magic outside of the Coven, Alyssa. You know that," Alice hissed.

This side of her brought back the words that I had heard as Victoria. Alice had tried to warn them of the hole in Alyssa. Alice. Not Anne. Not Victoria. Alice. So she knew that something was wrong with Alyssa. And that was why she had taken it upon herself to train her. It hadn't worked.

"Whose coven, Alice? I am a solitary witch as of last night. I need no coven."

Automatically both eyes shot to the circle burned into the floorboards. Alice's nostrils flared and her eyes blazed brightly. It was a clear reminder that Alice was made of flames. Fire was to her what music was to Alyssa and ivy was to me.

"The rite failed. You cannot lie to me, Alyssa. I know much about you. It's the reason I decided to train you when they allowed you into the Coven. I knew that I would fail with you. I just prayed that Fate had another destiny for you to be placed on. I was wrong. Stop practicing, Alyssa. If you don't, it will kill you."

Suddenly, without any indication, Alice turned on her heel and stalked out of the attic. Staring after her, I could not wipe the shocked look from my face. The same look was plastered all over Alyssa's. One *little warning. A warning no one but a witch would take seriously. A warning any other witch would have heeded. Not Alyssa.*

I found myself dragging in a ragged breath as I left the memory. My hand dropped, losing contact with the harp. I sensed one more memory in the room. Only one that would give away what else had happened. And yet, I knew that the pieces weren't enough. There had to be one way to get the full story, from the beginning. I just had to find it.

But the last memory had to come first. And it would be the hardest to stomach.

Inching my way to the vanity, I found my body shaking as I reached out my hand for the ornament. Magick pulsed in it and I knew that it held more than memories. Alyssa had stored power in it. Protective powers. Somehow, it had done her no good. And I would find out sooner than I wanted to.

Tremors shot through the attic as they had shot through

the room downstairs. Again, Victoria buffered them. Her face was expressionless as she stared after Alyssa.

"Keep doing that and the whole house will know that you're a witch." The voice she used was causal, cold, and cruel.

"You betrayed me, Victoria!" Alyssa snarled. "You were supposed to be my best friend forever. Instead you lied to me about magic our whole lives and then you turned your back on me when I began to grow more powerful than you."

Victoria looked almost bored as she replied. "If it had been only a week ago, Alyssa, I might have believed you. I might have doubted my abilities and succumbed to your forceful personality. Maybe I would have felt guilty over making you feel betrayed. Perhaps I'd even try to console you. Last week."

Victoria was a new person in my eyes. She sounded so much older than nine that it was scary. It was almost as if Alyssa's Rite of Ascension had bounced off of Alyssa and headed straight for her friend.

"But you betrayed us, Alyssa. Your lies and manipulations cannot hide it. Although I suppose I should thank you. Without your attempt at murder, I might never have gathered the nerve and taken the plunge. I thought there might be a river or lake at the end of the *fall. I was wrong. There's an ocean of power that I find myself consumed with. Were it not for the need to rein you in, I might never have found the absolute limitless energy I have filling me."*

"'Rein me in?'" Alyssa snarled. "And how do you propose to do that?"

"I'm going to bind your powers, Alyssa. The ritual is already begun. But you're too blind with rage to know what has just happened."

I was too blind with curiosity to realize what Victoria had been doing as well. Now that I took stock of everything, I soon realized what Alyssa had done for her.

Standing in the middle of the burnt circle was Alyssa. Standing on the northern edge, where Spirit would be in a pentagram, stood Victoria. All around, sand seemed to cover the circle again. It came from nowhere. Without our knowledge or notice. Like the ritual circle, the sand leached forward toward the center. Toward Alyssa.

Instead of stopping around her to create a circle, it continued to where it almost touched her feet. Gasping wildly, Alyssa leapt into the air and threw herself forcefully out of the circle. Even with the powerful barrier spells on it, Alyssa still broke free. The ornament glowed gold with her protection spells.

"You witch!" Alyssa snarled viciously at Victoria.

Victoria looked grimly at her best friend. And suddenly I knew that even though Victoria was doing what she had to, she still loved Alyssa like a sister. Appreciated her enough to want a better life for her. Cared enough to introduce her to magick and energy. Devoted enough to watch her back no matter what. Despite what was happening, Victoria loved Alyssa.

Loved her enough to kill her.

Chapter Forty One

MIRROR, MIRROR

My breathing was hard and I felt tears pooling in my eyes. I scrubbed them away viciously. Crying was about as taboo as screaming was for me. After blinking away the last of them, I turned my head to look about the room.

That was it? I thought woodenly. It couldn't have been. There was still so much missing.

My eyes trailed back to the vanity and the hairpiece that I had let drop to the table. Glancing at the mirror, I gasped and took a step back. Alyssa's haunting eyes stared out at me as if she knew what I was thinking.

Then I knew. The memories, the past experiences, the psychometry was all just a part of it. But only Alyssa could give me the full story. Only through her could I know what truly happened that awful night.

Without thought, I nodded to the image in the mirror. Stretching my hand out to touch the glass, I found myself whispering, "Mirror, mirror..."

I saw it all from the beginning. The day Alyssa met Victoria. The moment the two girls had become friends. Years of growing and playing together. Then the arrival of the rocking chair when they were about five.

Then came the ritual and the years of practice afterward. All of it whirled past me. I relived each memory I'd been previously shown. All of it leading up to the day that Alyssa died. There, I was given every single detail.

My fingers moved over the familiar keys. They were playing out a haunting, rich, exquisite melody. It was utterly magical. As I opened my eyes, even I was amazed by how fast my tiny fingers flew over the ivory keys. My ringlets fell across my shoulders as I was absorbed into the music. Life wound up in those transcending notes and got caught in the cordial pitches. I was sharing my heart and soul with those around me, all in the very sound of music.

Then the song ended on a haunting note and I looked up. The ivory dress flowed down to my knees as I stood up and bowed. I smiled in faux-appreciation. But I couldn't feel anything other than the desire to have them all gone. To just disappear and not come back.

That's when I saw her. My head turned, giving the same smile to the absolute strangers crowding my house, and I ended up spotting Victoria in the doorway. She wore her ritual dress. The one that was sapphire and flowing to the floor. In ritual she had a cloak over it, but it was the same dress that made her feel confident and powerful. Only I knew that.

The look on her face was expressionless, though the emotion in her eyes were whirling like a hurricane. Storms were rolling in within those eyes. Storms meant for me.

When she realized I had noticed her, we locked eyes and she motioned her head upwards to my room. I nodded slightly, feeling my teeth set on edge. She soon disappeared up the stairs to my room. And as soon as I could, I threw an invisible glamour over myself and followed her.

As soon as I entered my bedroom, I walked past

without even looking at her, using my magic to close the door behind me. Continuing to ignore her, I sat down in my chair and crossed my ankles, carefully folding my hands in my lap. I stared at those, willing myself not to do anything rash.

The urge to throw her out of the house was almost too great. Partially because I could feel the power rippling around her, drawing energy from every source available. A spark of jealousy stabbed through me.

Preparing myself mentally, I made sure to keep my features blank. Expressionless. Unreadable.

Then I looked up and my eyes bored into Victoria's the way her eyes were glaring into mine.

"What do you want, Victoria?" my voice was as chilled as ice.

"You know, they kill witches who betray their covens."

I hid my surprise at Victoria's even colder tone. How could she say that to me? Was she threatening me?

"I have no coven, Victoria. I betrayed no one."

"You used your power for evil, Alyssa. The most heinous evil. If that is not betrayal, then tell me what is."

My eyes suddenly burned with fire as I stared up at Victoria. "Betrayal is when the person who is supposed to be your best friend decides that she no longer wants anything to do with you once she realizes she's not as powerful."

"You think I am jealous of you, Alyssa?"

"Yes."

"You're wrong. I pity you," Victoria said in a silky, persuasive, cruel voice. It was a side to Victoria I had never seen before in all our lives.

"You're the one that deserves pity!" I spat the words.

"No. I don't have to be perfect for my parents to love me. And I don't have to be the most powerful in order to love myself. Perfect love and perfect trust, Alyssa. That is what you get when you enter a coven as you should. You can't handle that. And that's why you deserve my pity."

Tremors shot through the air, blurring the world inside of the bedroom. My rage was so strong that it could have leveled the house.

Almost instantly, a force built around the bedroom in order to contain them. I glared viciously at the witch who dared to try and stop me.

"We'll take this to the attic," I snarled. Victoria nodded in reply.

"Lead the way," she offered, holding out her hand.

I contained myself before throwing a glamour over my person. Victoria followed suit and we were soon headed for the attic.

Tremors shot through the attic as they had shot through the room downstairs. Again, Victoria buffered them. Her face was expressionless as she looked at me.

"Keep doing that and the whole house will know that you're a witch." The voice was casual, cold, and cruel. It set my teeth on edge.

"You betrayed me, Victoria!" I snarled. "You were supposed to be my best friend forever. Instead you lied to me about magic our whole lives and then you turned your back on me when I began to grow more powerful than you."

Victoria looked almost bored as she replied. "If it had been only a week ago, Alyssa, I might have believed you. I might have doubted my abilities and succumbed to your forceful personality. Maybe I would have felt guilty over making you feel betrayed. Perhaps I'd even try to console you. Last week."

Victoria was a new person in my eyes. She wasn't the weak, pathetic, afraid little girl I had known. She had changed. Grown. The power filling her expanded as she spoke.

"But you betrayed us, Alyssa. Your lies and manipulations cannot hide it. Although I suppose I should thank you. Without your attempt at murder, I might never have gathered the nerve and taken the plunge. I thought there might be a river or lake at the end of the fall. I was wrong. There's an ocean of power that I find myself consumed with. Were it not for the need to rein you in, I might never have found the absolute limitless energy I have filling me."

My rage was so much that I nearly tore her head off! So she found her ocean because of my flaws? NO! Victoria had no idea what real power was like. She was weak and pathetic. Just as she had always been.

"'Rein me in?' And how do you propose to do that?" Already I knew.

"I'm going to bind your powers, Alyssa. The ritual is already begun. But you're too blind with rage to know what has just happened."

I was too blind with anger to realize what Victoria had been doing. Now that I took stock of everything, I soon realized what I had stupidly done for her.

Standing in the middle of the burnt circle, I realized that Victoria was standing in the place of Spirit, the most powerful position in a pentagram. All around, sand seemed to cover the circle again. It came from nowhere. Without my knowledge or notice. Like the ritual circle, the sand leached forward toward the center. Toward me.

Instead of stopping around me to create a circle, it continued to where it almost touched my feet. Gasping wildly, I leapt into the air and threw myself forcefully out of the circle. Even with the powerful barrier spells on it, I was still able to break free. My ornament glowed gold with my protection spells and I could not be more grateful for them.

"You witch!" I snarled viciously at Victoria.

Victoria's expression was grim as she stared at me.

"You won't be needing this anymore," she stated calmly, reaching out her hand to touch my ornament. I shoved her hand out of the way and a struggle broke out between us.

The power coalescing around us as we fought was turning into a physical threat against one or the other of us. I remember my own wind blowing open the attic casements while Victoria's gift attempted to push me away. Furiously, I clung to my protective accessory while trying to inflict as much harm on my ex-best friend as I could.

Suddenly, the ornament flew out of my hands, getting tossed carelessly out the window. My eyes widened in fury as I turned to glare balefully at Victoria.

I found her panting from the fight, but with a triumphant little smile on her face.

Without thinking about it, I rushed at her with an inarticulate, guttural noise flying from my throat. My hands were claws prepared to rip out her eyes! There was red in my vision and I attacked her with magic even as I prepared to attack her physically.

I didn't realize it until it was too late. From the folds of her skirt, Victoria had pulled out a gleaming athame. The moonlight caught it just right as I hurtled toward her. My momentum could not be stopped and Victoria raised the blade.

The last sight I had was of her tears. They filled her eyes and coursed down her face. Victoria whispered, "I'm sorry, Alyssa." Her tears landed on my face.

For a child of fire, my last thought was of water.

Chapter Forty Two

NECESSARY MEMORIES

My mouth hung open and the tears fell down my face. Holding my stomach, I could almost feel myself bleeding out. Alyssa's death hadn't been quick. Hadn't been painless. And I hated myself for thinking, *That didn't make it any less necessary.*

I had started my journey in the hopes that I could make everything right for Alyssa. Now that I'd ended it, I found that it was necessary for her to die. She was too corrupt. The way she used magick was unbearable. If she had learned even more, I couldn't imagine how dangerous she would have become.

Victoria did what she had to.

With that thought, I was sucked back into the

mirror. This time, it wasn't because of Alyssa.

The athame dropped from my hands and I quickly caught my best friend. Without thinking about it, I dragged her into the circle and eased her to the ground. Alyssa stared at me with horrified eyes and I began to cry. I couldn't believe what I'd just done.

Time dragged on as my poor friend's blood eased out of her body and traveled into the burn mark before disappearing entirely. Even magic was helping to erase the memory of Alyssa Rice. Finally, after an hour, Alyssa took her last gasp and a single tear rolled down her cheek to land on my dress. At last, she closed her eyes and sank into the world of spirits.

I crumpled over top of her, rocking her and sobbing into her clothes. No little girl should have to endure this. The sight of death. The killing of her best friend. Knowing what it feels like to take a life.

Alyssa's hole, the part that made her dark, opened inside my chest. As if she had passed her hunger for power to me, it sat there, eating at all positive emotion. Unlike Alyssa, however, I was not fire. I was water. I knew how to cradle disaster with blessings. I could carry both within me for all of time. Alyssa could only consume, consume, consume. She would forever fail to fill that hole. And I would hold it inside until the day that I died.

A broken scream filled the night, causing my head to snap up. Alyssa's mother. They'd noticed her disappearance.

The magic cleared my thoughts, pushing them away to think logically. The blood of Alyssa had seeped into the universe, leaving even her dress spotless. It was as if Alyssa had bled into the house itself, refusing to leave where her own roots would forever lie.

Leaping to my feet, I snatched the key from where Alyssa had dropped it. She always kept the thing on her. Then I rushed down the stairs and locked the attic door, placing her snow globe back on its shelf. Afterward, I hurried back up the stairs.

Magick was my ally. And in a way, so was Alyssa. By making her rocking chair trade places with her trunk, she gave me what I needed to preserve her body right there in the attic. The key to this was always on Alyssa as well.

Opening the lock with the golden key, the chest flew open to reveal all of Alyssa's ritual belongings. Oh yes, this was the perfect place to lay her to rest. With all of the things that were sacred to her.

Using my newly strengthened powers, I picked up Alyssa and placed her in the chest. Then I did the hardest thing I had to do—other than killing her—I closed the lid on the chest and replaced the lock. My heart broke as I did it. The key practically burned in my pocket. But it had to be done.

The windows were still open and a sudden vision of a gothic door hit me. Again using the magic I hadn't known I had so much control over, I eased the chest off the attic floor and floated it out the window. Slowly, ever so slowly, I lowered it to the ground. Then, as might have been predicted, I leapt gracefully out of the window, lowering myself to the ground as gently as possible.

I stood outside the brick house beside the small, gothic-arched wooden door that looked older than any other part of the building. Ivy grew around it and I wondered why it had never grown over it before. No one had used it in years.

Looking down at my tiny hands, I suddenly wanted to vomit. How could such little things be tools of murder? Choking back bile, I reached into the ivy where a brick was always loose. It was where the key was hidden. Pulling it out, I opened the door and allowed the trunk with Alyssa's body to float into the *tiny crevice.*

With tears in my eyes, I muttered a sealing spell, in order to keep the trunk from opening until such time as Alyssa was able to move on to the other world. Even now, I could feel her ghostly presence surrounding me. Watching me as I hid her from the world. Then I closed and locked the door.

At that point, I pulled out all three keys. The keys that would hide Alyssa and any memory of her. After staring at them, my right hand closed over them and placed them in my pocket. Afterward, I took a shaking step back to say the necessary spell.

"Hide my secrets, and hide them well.
Let none know I've cast this spell.
This secret is not meant to be shared.
Not one person shall be spared.
I call on thee to hide from me,
This door so that none shall see.
Close it up.
Make it disappear.
Let none find it.
Not even under deepest fear.
So mote it be."

Like a heavy curtain being let loose from its bindings, the ivy adorning the house unfurled itself and began to drape over the door. From the ground, more green shoots sprouted in response to my need. In a mere moment's time, the ivy had hidden away all there was to see. None would ever know to look beneath the vines.

Nodding once to myself, I turned and walked away.

I would never stop gasping. Not after this story. Something was lodged in my throat as I tried to put into words what I'd just seen. But I couldn't. There were no words to describe what I had witnessed. A mystery from the past had finally been revealed. I now knew the whole story of what happened to Alyssa Mae Rice.

And yet, I still had no way to get to her. Only one key was in my possession. And yet, I knew right where the other two were, as though Alyssa were whispering their locations in my mind.

Maybe it was cocky of me, but I did as Victoria had done. I locked the attic door from the inside, the snow globe safely on its shelf. And then I opened the southern window. The one that led to the backyard.

Levitation allowed for a body to move upwards. Or downwards, if you did it right. Slowly, I climbed out of the third story window and let the power surge through me. Victoria was lucky. It was dark when she did this. She didn't have to see how far down the ground was.

Closing my eyes, I concentrated on feeling as light as the air. I had no weight. The air was more solid than I was. Then a breeze blew harmlessly around me as I thought of descending to the ground and my stomach dropped. Suddenly, my feet hit the grassy lawn and I opened my eyes while grinning widely.

Almost immediately it was wiped from my face. Just knowing what my task entailed...

I knew where the door was. I'd seen it enough in memory in order to be able to place its exact location on the house. Slowly, tentatively, I laced my fingers through the ivy. Were it not *my* trigger, I doubt my hand would have made it through. But it did and I soon felt ancient wood beneath my searching fingers. I gulped.

Suddenly, a spell found its way into my head.

"Part now so that I may see.
Show me Alyssa's destiny.
Part now from my way.
Show me what the past showed me today.
Be gone from my path.
Be gone from around my hand.
Be gone from this door.
Retreat forever more."

Suddenly, the ivy began to inch away, pulling into the sides where the other vines held tightly to them. Revealed to me was a gothic-arched door.

Stepping close, I placed my hand into the crevice Victoria had found the key in.

It was empty.

Chapter Forty Three

KEYS TO THE PAST

My heart sank. Where could it be? Obviously Victoria had not put it where anyone might possibly remember the door's existence. So where, then?

I spun in place, looking out over the yard. There was nothing. Nothing special about it that would make it worth hiding outside. Biting my lip, I walked around the house. Around and around I paced. Suddenly, as I reached the front of the house, I tripped on the stepping stone walkway.

The rocks dug into my skin, ripping a hole in my jeans. *That* I didn't care about. I was used to gaining holes in my clothes.

But there was a cut that was deep enough to be running with blood. Rolling up my pant leg, I came to see what it really looked like. There was one decent gash and the blood ran down my leg in thin little tendrils. With wide eyes, I lifted my head to stare directly at the garden gate. The witches hazel danced in the wind. Mocking me.

Getting to my feet, I inched closer to the yellow shrub. The roses beside it seemed to grow bigger in my eyes. And I knew. Right then I knew where the key was.

Witches hazel was planted in olden days in the hopes to keep witches away. It was planted here by Victoria, I was sure. Next to the roses that always symbolized Alyssa Rice. She was blocking Alyssa's influence, even in death. Victoria was protecting everyone from her best friend and almost-sister.

Sitting beneath the shrub, I felt the yellow flowers brush at my hair. It was a miracle they'd survived so late into the autumn. The roses, too, were almost supernaturally kept in place. The effects of magick from two separate little girls.

There, beneath the witches hazel and clinging to a single, fully blooming wild rose was the key. The brass key that was bound to both plants, keeping the secret of the past well hidden. With a surging feeling of rightness, I reached out my hand tentatively and removed it from its hiding place. Finally, Alyssa would be free.

I didn't take the key back to the door. Not yet. There was still one key I had yet to get. Sticking it in my pocket, I marched through my front door and entered the parlor.

Of course Victoria would place the last key in the one object she knew would never leave Alyssa's house. The piano. The golden gleam I had seen oh so long ago had a new meaning now. I knew what it was. And I knew how to get it.

Telekinesis allowed me to lift the piano lid and hold it in place. At the same time, the small, gold trinket released itself from its bindings and floated up to land in my hands. I snatched it from the air and allowed the piano lid to close. Turning on my heel, I headed back outside to the small door that was Alyssa's prison.

I don't think I was honestly prepared for what I was going to find. But at least I had an inkling. So, with the air of determined, curious young witch, and with a lot of Ryder Pride, I placed the key into the lock on the gothic-arched door.

It turned so easily one might not have believed that it hadn't been touched in nearly eighty years.   Gulping once more, I eased it open.

There, in the tiny little room, was the chest that reminded me of pirate treasure. Old-fashioned tools hung on the walls and a shelf held old broken pottery and small shovels. It was basically a gardening shed at one point. And no one had used it in Victoria's time because they had actually built the shed at that point. It was the perfect place to hide Alyssa.

"I don't mean to intrude, and disturb your rest, Alyssa. But I have to set you free somehow," I whispered before taking a step into the room.

Holding my breath, I kneeled down and put the key in the lock. I heard the defining click as the latch opened. Removing the padlock, I slowly lifted the lid, keeping my head averted and holding my breath.

When I first looked, Alyssa looked just how I had seen her in the memories. Her ivory dress was spotless and her skin looked the picture of health. She looked as if she were merely sleeping. For only a moment.

As I watched, the body began to decay before my eyes. I gagged and covered my mouth, turning away from the trunk. I'd never seen a dead person before. And that was one of the most horrifying things I had ever seen in my life.

Suddenly, I looked up and saw Alyssa Rice. Not nine-year-old Alyssa. The twenty-year-old Alyssa she had tried to force herself into being. The person she always wished her magick could make her. I saw *her*. She smiled at me.

"Thank you, Lex." The words resounded in my head and I nodded numbly. Then Alyssa faded from existence.

Somehow, she had settled a calm over me. Knowing that I really had helped Alyssa was enough. She wasn't trapped anymore. Alyssa was free and that, at least, helped to wipe away some of the horror of her remains.

Turning silently, I walked into the back door and went straight to our junk drawer in the kitchen. The Cedar Creek phone book wasn't very thick and I pulled it out with ease. Grabbing the phone off the wall, I set it beside me as I opened the phone book. Good thing emergency services was toward the front.

Dialing swiftly, I waited as a voice came over the line. "Cedar Creek Police Station."

"Hi, I'd like to report a found human body at 03 Verity Lane."

For a moment the person on the other end was completely silent and I imagined they were tracing the call. Obviously they were wondering if this nine-year-old kid was pulling a prank or not. I almost sighed.

"What is your name?"

"Alexandria Ryder. I currently live at 03 Verity Lane," I answered calmly.

"How old are you Alexandria?"

"Nine."

"And just to confirm: you say that you have found human remains on your property?"

"Yes."

"Can you identify the remains in question?"

"Yes. Although you won't believe me until you see for yourselves."

"Why is that?"

"Because the body is that of Alyssa Mae Rice. The girl who disappeared in 1922."

Again, the woman on the other end went completely silent. For a few seconds nothing was said. This time I really did sigh into the phone.

"If you have no more questions, I'm going to go tell my mother that you're on your way." I hung up.

Quietly, I padded to the office where my mother was typing something on her computer. Probably getting new project ideas for her high schoolers. After standing in the doorway for a minute, I cleared my throat. She looked at me in surprise.

"Hey baby. Oh goodness! What happened?" she panicked when she saw my leg. I looked down, totally forgetting about the bleeding gash.

"Don't worry about it. I'll douse it with peroxide soon. Listen, Mom," I said, interrupting her next freak out, "there's something I have to tell you. I ... I found a body. A human one. The cops will be here any minute to question me. I just thought you should know."

My mother's mouth dropped as she stared at me with wide eyes. I wished there was a way to get her over the shock. Instead, we stood there looking at one another for several long, *long* minutes. Suddenly, a pounding on the front door snapped her out of it. Just as I was turning for the front door, Mom put her hand on my shoulder, giving me that determined mother-bear look.

"*I'll* get it," she informed me and moved past me to the front door. I stood quietly in the background.

"Hello, ma'am. We've gotten a report of human remains being found on your property. Do you have a nine-year-old daughter named Alexandria?"

Oh great, I thought. The idiots didn't take me seriously and sent a couple of goons to take care of the misdemeanor phone call. I rolled my eyes and stepped up to my mother.

"I am Alexandria."

"Lex," my mother hissed and I looked at her meaningfully. Then I turned back to the police officers.

"Follow me," I ordered, moving past them. Exchanging surprised looks, the two cops and my mother all followed me out of the house. I led them around to the back of the house where the door was still wide open.

I gagged again as I noticed the swarm of flies already moving in to claim Alyssa's flesh. Turning, I clung to my mother.

"Oh my God!" I heard her whisper as she used one hand to cover her mouth while the other hand pressed my head to her abdomen.

"Dear God!" one officer exclaimed.

The other, older, officer was already on his radio, ordering vehicles and teams of all sorts. Afterward, he cleared his throat and motioned that we should head inside away from the scene.

"Mrs. Ryder, I assume your husband would like to be made aware of the situation."

"Yes, of course. Lex, why don't you call your father?" Point one for Mom. She knew not to let me talk to the officer on my own. Also, it was my place to call Dad.

After hanging up the phone with him, I found my mother and the cop sitting at the kitchen table. The other cop was outside directing the other people to Alyssa's resting place. They were trampling the garden and it upset me. But it was Alyssa's garden. And they were trampling it to get to her. So I had to give a little on that front.

"Alexandria. Your mother and I were just discussing your findings. On the phone you identified the body as Alyssa Rice. You didn't tell your mother this?"

My mom held out her arms to me and I sat in her lap. I felt safe and secure. At the same time, I felt older than her. As though the memories had aged me. The power had aged me. It was her who needed protecting from this situation. Not me.

"No. I don't want to talk about this. I *won't* talk about this anymore."

"Alexandria, you made the phone call that brought us here. We need all of the information we can get so that we can find this little girl's identity and give her some rest."

"I gave her rest the moment I found her body. Your only job is to give her a proper burial. You don't need me for that."

"Alexandria!" my mother admonished, turning her head to look at me. "He's only trying to help. Tell him what you know."

I shook my head. "No. I'm not talking about Alyssa Rice. She's at rest now and I don't want to think about her anymore."

Suddenly, I stood up from my mother's lap and ran outside. My dad was just getting out of his car and I ran straight to his arms. Here was my ally. The one person I could count on to respect my wishes. No matter how they defied everyone else's.

"Oh my Lexi Girl," he murmured as he lifted me up and cradled me in his arms.

Together, for the rest of the night, Dad and I fought off question after question thrown at us by investigators and even by my mom. I didn't want to talk about what was happening and no one could make me. Dad made sure of that— though he used the common excuse of childhood trauma. If only he knew what was really keeping me quiet about the whole situation...

Chapter Forty Four

BALANCING BOTH WORLDS

"**M**edical Examiners confirm that the body of Alyssa Rice—the young musician who disappeared at her own celebration in 1922—has been found."

"To add to the mystery surrounding this disturbing discovery, Nancy, we now know that it was a young girl, Alexandria Ryder, to discover the body. Now, there's a lot of speculation going around, but since Alexandria refuses to answer any questions regarding the matter, it can be most easily guessed at that she was just playing in the yard and happened upon the door that police say was hidden from sight at the time of Alyssa's disappearance."

"Right you are, Robert. And mind you, the mystery grows when we add in the strange circumstances that seem to link these two girls. I'm not sure if you've noticed, Rob, but both girls share the same initials: A. M.

R. and at this time Alexandria Ryder is nine years old. The very same age Alyssa Rice disappeared at. Living in the same house, they even have the same bedroom, sources say."

"That is correct, Nancy. Sources also report that in the chest holding Alyssa's body were a number of supplies we now identify with the Wiccan religion. Could Alyssa really have reached through time to touch the girl who was so much like her? We may never know."

"As you've said, Rob, speculation is all we have. Stay tuned to—"

I turned the TV off in disgust. Whoever their source was, they were going to hear it from me if I ever found out who they were. Alyssa's discovery had turned into some ridiculous media frenzy. I was just grateful they seemed stumped as to the cause of death. They'd already determined that she was dead before being placed into the chest. Something about how *rigor mortis* had set in prior to her body being moved to its current position.

Sighing, I stood up and stretched. Slowly, I walked to my mother's office. She and dad were talking in low voices again. It didn't take a genius to know that they were arguing. Mom really wanted to know what had led me to find her. Dad argued against pushing me.

I almost knocked on the door. Almost. Instead of disturbing my parents' argument, I headed for the stairs. I had a feeling nothing would ever be the same between Mom and I again. And some-day, when Dad learned the truth, things would become even more strained between all of us. But was giving up my powers worth never upsetting my parents? Absolutely not.

Vaguely I realized that I was dreaming. I was back at Morgan's, but it was different. The stone walls were neglected and had soot covering them in thick layers. Baby clothes lay over top of furniture and everything was coated in dust.

Turning, I found a twenty-three-year-old Victoria holding baby Morgan in her arms. They were rocking away in Alyssa's rocking chair. I assumed that Alyssa's mother had given it to her daughter's best friend. That would explain its move from one house to the other.

Suddenly, the door burst open and a dark figure loomed over her. Again, I saw the fear in her eyes. It was squelched the moment the dark figure materialized into Anne. Alice followed afterward.

Slowly, Victoria pushed to her feet. After crooning to the fussing baby, she scanned each of their faces. I had the feeling that her mother had died, causing the lack of order to the house and the sudden confrontation of the twins. For a moment, I was surprised that they had come. That they had waited so long. And why were they alone?

A few minutes more made me realize that the night of Alyssa's death had also been the last night of the Coven. She had truly broken them all apart. Suspicion and fear of betrayal had blanketed them so fully on the night of her disappearance. Such mistrust could never be forgotten. So the Coven had faded away. And only Alice knew why.

Now, with the protection of her mother gone, the twins had come. One to exact revenge for a broken family. Anne. The other to administer justice, though she knew well that what Victoria did was for the good of them all. Alice.

"Alice, will you raise her?" Victoria asked in a steady, calm voice.

"Why me?"

"Because you always see the truth of things. Even when others do not. After all, you, alone, know what

truly happened between us that night. Now it is your burden to bear that you will leave my daughter without her mother. So it is you who shall raise her."

"I accept the responsibility," Alice said in a chill voice as Victoria handed her the child. Victoria nodded and turned to Anne.

"I accept the responsibility for killing Alyssa Rice. Witness and perform the justice to be done. Take me to the lake."

I wasn't the only one surprised with her calm determination. Slowly, they drifted out of the house and marched along the dirt road to the lake at the end.

I thought I was going to cry. Victoria stood on the banks of the river and let her raven hair out of the braid. Anne stood behind her and brushed it to a smooth black curtain. Victoria smiled and she took off her clothes and slid on the ceremonial dress. It was blue and the moonlight on the water set off all of the silver flecks.

Turning one last time, Victoria blew a kiss to her daughter. Then she turned her back on her and walked into the water. As her toes entered the silt, her voice rang out high, calling on the elements of earth and water to pull her down into the depths and hold her there until justice was done.

Bit by bit, Victoria disappeared into her watery grave. The gentle laps of the lake made it seem as untouched as before. Like magick hadn't caused it to take a life. Minute after minute, I kept expecting Victoria's body to float to the surface.

It never did.

"Is that it, then? Are all the questions answered?" Morgan asked as we walked through the trees. We were strolling around in the garden, taking in the beauty and calm.

"Not all. Why was I shown Mary Sullivan's burning during my Wiccaning?"

"That one is a question for you to answer on your own one day. I know little of her and you seem to have a direct link with the past. I am sure you will figure it out."

"I wish that would happen sooner rather than later," I grumbled in defeat.

"Where there are questions, there is always a never-ending story."

We turned toward the bench at that point. I was suddenly surprised to find Nathan at the gate, his hands tucked into his jacket pockets.

Though he looked nervous, I sensed that he was waiting for me. Looking at Morgan in confusion, she smiled at me.

"It's about time you learn to balance all parts of both worlds, Lex. Go. Enjoy yourselves."

I shook my head in amusement. "Thank you, Morgan. I will see you later."

Silently, as was our habit, Nathan and I walked to the end of Old Grove Road where a lake was dug into the earth, holding mystery upon mystery beneath its glassy surface.

ACKNOWLEDGEMENTS

Next to Author Bios, Acknowledgments are the hardest to do. Between all the people who help to create a novel and those that simply push the author to do the thing, there are a lot of people to be grateful for.

Firstly, I have to thank my sister, Mariah. If she had not become so enraptured by the tale of this little witch, I don't know when or if I ever would have made it this far. Thank you, Sister.

As far as the process of taking this story from manuscript to book, the person who has done the most is Christiana Nehmsmann. We often joke that she is the mother of my book children; I provide a lump sum of material and she transforms it into something other people can enjoy. She's my best friend and one of the few people I absolutely could not live without. Having taken the time to recreate all new covers, design the interiors, and provide all of the support I could otherwise need, I know this series would not exist without this woman. Thank you so much for all you do, and all that you've put up with from me. I love you!

My grandparents, Leah and Marvin, have always been the most supportive of my writing and have pushed me the most. I don't even know how to thank you both, but I will try to say it here: Thank you. I'm so proud to be your granddaughter.

As far as spouses go, I got one of the best ones. Christopher doesn't read my work under threat of violence, and he only rarely tries to sneak a peek. In the early stages of our relationship, he got to witness Writer Brain more times than he thought possible and he rode it out like a champ. Thank you, honey, for listening to all my crazy newly-learned facts, nodding through all my rants, and otherwise letting me be as crazy as I am without judgment. I love you.

Honorable mentions for the rest of my

family: Jamie and Juduk, Travis and Maria, and all the Littles. Thank you for all of the support and love. Even though we're all far apart, you're all close in my heart. I love you... (You know the rest, but it's your saying so I won't put it in print.)

Last, but definitely not least, to my mommy: thank you for defending me and my beliefs. Thank you for your support and your understanding. I couldn't do any of this without you. I love you the most. Always will.

ABOUT THE AUTHOR

Hollow Ryan is a Michigan native with thirty years spent too much in her own head, and twenty years putting it all on paper. This obsession with the written word has led her to publish the five-book paranormal series, *The Prideful Magick Collection*. It has also started her on a journey full of *Demon Kin*.

When not working on her ever-expanding Work List, Hollow is dealing with the three most spoiled fur-children to be found in Northeastern Michigan. (Her spouse is absolutely to blame for that.)

For more information, please visit:
www.hollowryan.com

Chapter One

TRUTH

"The Defense calls Alexandria Ryder to the stand."

I tried to convince myself that I was prepared for this, while my heart tried to hammer its way out of my ribcage. The pounding of my pulse sounded like tribal drums in my ears as adrenaline flooded my bloodstream. Fight or flight?

My legs were unsteady underneath me and I locked my knees as soon as I stood up. Taking a deep breath, I forced one foot in front of the other as I crossed the open space in front of the jury. When I made it to the witness stand, I stepped up in front of the chair and raised my right hand as instructed.

"Do you swear to tell the truth, the whole

truth, and nothing but the truth?"

"I do."

"You may be seated."

It took every inch of willpower I had not to fall into that chair. When I was seated, I made sure to keep both feet firmly on the floor to keep my knee from bouncing. As I took in this new view of the courtroom, I found that I wasn't nearly as prepared as I had thought.

Surreal. It shouldn't have seemed that way, but it was. Like it could have been happening in a dream, or to someone else. How could this be happening to me?

The lawyer approached, her light hair gathered in a bun at the back of her head, jade eyes filled with purpose whilst her expression remained free of her thoughts. "Please state your name and age for the court." It wasn't a question.

"Alexandria Ryder. Fourteen."

I didn't realize how difficult it was to breathe until I had to speak. For one, long second, I took a deep breath and held it. When I exhaled, I tried to force all of the nerves out at the same time. It helped a little.

"Miss Ryder, why are you testifying here

today?"

"I want people to know the truth."

"Couldn't they learn it by the evidence being presented or the other statements presented?"

"No."

"Why not?"

The way she spoke was calm and inquisitive. Far from our first encounter with one another. Much had occurred since that day, and I found her presence more soothing than frustrating. Which was why the last of my nerves vanished as we talked, forgetting everything around us and what it meant in the long run.

"There are a dozen ways to interpret evidence. I've seen it firsthand in this very courtroom. What cannot be misinterpreted, however, is what I saw. Felt. Experienced. I know what happened, because I was there. Since the evidence can't say it plain, it's up to me to tell everyone what happened."

Her blue-green eyes narrowed in warning. In a voice laden with false suspicion, she demanded, "Why should we believe you?"

There is a fine line between truth and magick.

If every person in that room knew anything about magick, they would no longer know what was truth or lie. Illusion or revelation. Should any person come to know that everything I said was possible, they would no longer believe in the impossible.

They would never believe that it was impossible for me to murder someone I loved.

"I have no reason to lie."

"There are those that would beg to differ."

"They're wrong."

"Then prove it. Tell us what happened. Make us believe you."

Even as her words settled into my skin, a white mist rose up before my eyes, taking me back to this day one year ago.